Poppy's Prayers
Book 8 in Clover Creek Community
Kirsten Osbourne

Chapter One

June 1866

Inside the one-room schoolhouse in Clover Creek, Poppy leaned over a small desk. Her fingers were stained with ink as she corrected a young boy's arithmetic, her dedication to education evident in every carefully chosen word of encouragement.

"Remember now, Timothy," she said softly, "you have to be careful where you place your numbers. If you carry the one in the wrong place, you'll never get the right answer."

As her students packed their slates and readers, Poppy's gaze lingered out the window. She harbored dreams as vast as the Oregon Trail itself, dreams where every child in her care would carry the light of knowledge across the untamed land.

Meanwhile, a lone figure approached the burgeoning town of Clover Creek. Jacob Alexander rode a sturdy chestnut horse, its hooves kicking up clouds of dust along the dirt road. His dark hair was swept back from a face that bore the marks of hardship, and his eyes, a deep brown, surveyed the town with apprehension.

Jacob had journeyed far to reach this place, carrying with him the heavy burden of loss. The ghosts of his brother and the war they fought together clung to him. But Clover Creek promised a whole new beginning. Here, he would start a new life and build a dairy farm that would support him and his future family.

Dismounting in front of the town's general store, he took a deep breath, glad no one here knew him or his past. He didn't need people trying to comfort him about the loss of his twin brother. He needed to begin again, not forgetting, but not dwelling on the past either. Clover

Creek, filled with mountains and beautiful Bear Lake was right where he needed to be. He was certain of it.

The woman behind the counter in the store held a baby on one hip as she helped another customer with her purchases. Then her eyes landed on Jacob. "Hello. I don't think we've met yet. I'm Penelope Jensen."

Jacob nodded. "Jacob Alexander. I have claimed some land near town. I'm starting a dairy farm."

The storekeeper gave an approving nod. "We could use more dairy farms around here. It's good land and even better people." She smiled. "Welcome to Clover Creek."

Jacob nodded. "It's good to finally be here. I ended up wintering in Oregon City, and I just kept thinking about all the time I was wasting."

"Welcome to Clover Creek, Mr. Alexander," Mrs. Jensen said with a genuine smile. "I hope you'll find what you're looking for here."

Jacob hoped the woman was right. The idea of a new beginning made him feel happier than he had in a long time.

POPPY SMITH'S FINGERS danced across the ivory keys of an old organ, coaxing out a hymn that filled the space with tranquility that seemed almost tangible. The notes rose and fell, a delicate echo of the peaceful Sunday morning, as the congregation followed her lead in song.

Poppy's red hair was pinned back neatly, but a few rebellious curls had escaped. Her eyes closed gently with each chord she played, her face the very picture of serene devotion. As the last note lingered in the air, there was a stillness that settled over the room.

The service concluded with Pastor Jed Scott offering a benediction, his voice warm and comforting. As the congregation began to disperse, exchanging quiet words and nods, the pastor made his way to where Jacob Alexander stood somewhat apart from the others.

"Jacob," Jed greeted him, his hand extended in welcome. "I trust this morning finds you well?"

"Yes, it does, Pastor," Jacob replied, his handshake firm.

"Come, let me introduce you to someone," Jed said, guiding Jacob toward the piano where Poppy was gathering her sheet music. "Miss Poppy Smith, our local schoolteacher and very talented musician meet Mr. Jacob Alexander, new to our community and planning to start a dairy farm."

Poppy looked up, her green eyes meeting Jacob's dark gaze, a spark of curiosity igniting as their hands met in a brief but firm handshake.

"Mr. Alexander," she said. "Welcome to Clover Creek. I hope you find this town the answer to all your dreams, as I do."

"Thank you, Miss Smith," Jacob responded. "I've claimed a little piece of land just outside of town. There's a furniture builder not far from me."

Poppy grinned. "That furniture builder is my brother-in-law. I live with him and my older sister and their children."

"Perhaps you'd like to join us for our noon meal?" Jed interjected, sensing the potential for a deeper connection. "Hannah and I are always happy to get to know new people coming to settle here."

Jacob hesitated. He wasn't used to being welcomed warmly. "I'd be honored," he finally said.

"Excellent!" Jed clapped his hands together. "It's settled then."

As the two men walked away, Poppy found herself watching Jacob, a sense of anticipation stirring within her. There was a story behind those eyes. She loved to meet new people and hear their stories. Sometimes, she even wrote them down to amuse herself.

WHEN POPPY RETURNED to her sister Sarah's home, she helped get the little ones fed. After more than ten years of marriage, Sarah had five children, and Poppy did all she could to help her sister.

"Elmer invited our new neighbor for supper tonight," Sarah told her. "He seems like a very nice man." Sarah was well aware that her sister was interested in getting married and starting a family of her own.

"Oh, I met him after the service today. Pastor Jed introduced him. His eyes seem to be aching to tell a story. I can't wait to hear it." She wondered if all the prayers she'd been saying daily since finishing school were leading her to Jacob Alexander. She prayed for a husband and family every day.

Sarah smiled. "I'll find some way to leave the two of you alone at least for a little bit. Then you can get to know each other and decide what you think of him."

Poppy's whole face lit up at the idea. "I would love that if you don't mind."

Sarah shook her head. "With all the help you've given me with my children over the years, I could never pay you back for what you've done."

"You raised me. You could have easily sent the three of us to live with another family, but you never considered the option. I will never stop being grateful to you."

Sarah shook her head. "I couldn't very well leave my brothers and sister."

Poppy smiled. She could never get Sarah to understand what a wonderful thing she'd done without making her sister uncomfortable. "Is it okay if I work in the garden for a bit? I want to sink my hands in the dirt."

Sarah laughed. "You think you need my permission to help me garden?"

Poppy smiled at that before going to her room to change into some old clothes. She'd be sure to change again before Mr. Alexander arrived for supper.

An hour later, she was kneeling in the dirt, carefully pulling weeds from the garden. She could feel a smudge of dirt across her face, and she knew she looked a fright.

When it was time to help Sarah with supper, Poppy stood and brushed as much dirt off her dress as she could. She would change right away, of course, but she didn't want to get dirt all over Sarah's clean home.

"Miss Smith?" The voice was deep, slightly roughened. Jacob Alexander stood there, watching her brush the dirt from her dress. "Is this how the schoolteacher spends her Sunday afternoons?"

"Mr. Alexander," Poppy replied, her voice steady despite the fluttering in her chest. Her gaze met his, and for an instant, she felt like she would never be able to catch her breath. She wished she knew the secrets hidden in the deep pools of his brown eyes, but she wasn't certain he would ever let her close enough to know anything.

"Jacob, please," he said, closing the distance between them with a few measured steps. "I hope I'm not late."

"Of course not." She smiled. "I was just about to go inside and help Sarah with supper. My brother-in-law is in his furniture shop. Would you like me to take you there?"

"Yes, I'd like to see his work." They walked side by side to the building beside their home, their arms barely grazing. Each brush was like a spark that spread through Poppy's body. "Have you always been a teacher, Miss Smith?" Jacob asked.

"Poppy, please," she corrected gently. "And yes, I've been teaching since I turned sixteen four years ago. We had a lot of teachers in and out before that. I love watching young faces light up when they learn something new."

"Admirable," he murmured, his gaze lingering on her.

"Elmer, you remember Jacob Alexander."

Elmer looked up from a rocking chair he was sanding. "Good to see you again, Jacob."

"I'll leave the two of you. I need to help Sarah with supper." Poppy left, immediately going to talk to Sarah. "I'm covered in dirt, and he's here. I'm going to change into something cleaner, and then I'll help with supper."

Sarah smiled. "You look beautiful as always."

"Don't flatter me. I know the sheer amount of dirt I'm wearing."

"You may want to wash your face while you're changing. There's dirt smeared." Sarah pointed to her chin, and then her forehead. "Well, really, it's all over."

Poppy closed her eyes for a moment. "And this is the first eligible man I've found to be attractive. Of course, I'm covered in dirt." She hurried from the room and cleaned up, coming back in one of the dresses she wore to teach. Wasn't it just her luck to meet a kind man when she was wearing more dirt than the Oregon Trail?

Sarah had decided on chicken and dumplings for supper. Many of the townsfolk needed furniture, but it was easier for them to pay with chickens or hogs. Sarah based many of their meals on the currency Elmer was paid in.

"Who gave us the chickens?" Poppy asked, knowing that's why they were having this particular meal."

"Pastor Jed and Hannah," Sarah said. "They received the chickens as a tithe, and Hannah needed another bed. Her children are growing up so quickly."

Poppy smiled. "It's hard to believe I teach them." Poppy rolled out the dough for the dumplings while her sister put the chicken into the pot and added water and spices. Together, they'd made many meals, and they had a rhythm down.

"Jack and Grace will be here for supper tonight as well as Charles."

"Oh, good. We'll have a full house. It's a good thing Elmer made such a long table."

After cutting the dough for the dumplings, Poppy put them in a bowl and worked on cleaning up the table. It was covered with flour from their cooking endeavors.

When it was finally time for the meal, Poppy went to tell Elmer and Jacob. "It's time to eat." She wasn't at all surprised to see Jacob helping sand the chair Elmer was making.

Both men got to their feet. "What are we having?" Elmer asked.

"Chicken and dumplings."

Elmer looked at Jacob. "I'm sorry, but there's not going to be enough food for you."

Jacob smiled, shaking his head. "Not even one bite?"

"Not by the time I'm done," Elmer said, leading the way into the house.

Jacob enjoyed watching Poppy walk to the house in front of them. She was slender and pretty. He could marry a girl like her.

When they got to the dining room, everyone took their seat. Poppy helped get all the food on the table, and then she automatically bowed her head for the prayer. Elmer's prayer thanked God for bringing Jacob to them and said he hoped they would become fast friends.

Throughout the meal, conversation ebbed and flowed around them. Laughter and the clinking of cutlery filled the room, but beneath the din, a silent exchange unfolded between Poppy and Jacob. Each time their eyes met, words seemed unnecessary.

When talk turned to Jacob's plans for a dairy farm, his answers were concise, painting a picture of toil and dedication. Yet, there lurked shadows behind his words, spaces where details should have been. Poppy listened intently, trying her very best to understand the man.

"What do you think of Clover Creek? Is it a great deal different from wherever you're from?" Poppy asked.

"Change is necessary sometimes," Jacob responded. "Survival requires adaptation." His gaze drifted to the window. For a moment, his expression was veiled, hinting at a history marked by loss.

"It is," Poppy agreed softly, wishing she knew what brought the sadness into his eyes. "Sometimes survival is the only thing possible for a while, until we can learn to be happy again."

As the evening waned, and guests began to depart, Sarah suggested Poppy make sure Jacob knew the way back to the boarding house.

Poppy was certain Jacob knew her sister was trying to get them alone for a few minutes, but he didn't say anything about it, and neither did she.

"How long do you think you'll be staying at the boarding house?" she asked.

Jacob shrugged. "I'm not sure. When I got to town on Friday, I ordered lumber for a house and a barn. I think as soon as I get the basic house built, I can move out there. It'll be summer, and there's no reason I can't live with the bare necessities." He looked at her. "You really like living here, don't you?"

She nodded. "I remember being so scared when I was a little girl and we left Independence, and I was right to be scared. We lost both of our parents on the trail, which is why Sarah and Elmer had to raise us. But since we've settled here, everything seems just a little bit better. How could someone ever wake up with the view here and not feel they were in the most beautiful place God created?"

He smiled, but it failed to reach his eyes. "I hope it's like that for me as well. I love it here so far."

"I do as well. I don't see myself ever leaving Clover Creek. At this point, it's all I know."

"Would you mind if I walked you home from school tomorrow?" he asked. He wanted to spend his time focusing on his farm, but she seemed like a likely candidate for a wife. He wanted children soon. He had no other family now that his brother had passed, and he didn't like knowing he was the last of his blood.

"I'd like that," she said with a smile. Perhaps he was as attracted to her as she was to him. She liked the idea.

"I'll see you at four then," he said with a smile and a wave, as he hurried away toward the boarding house. As he walked, his mind was still on Poppy. "She'll do. She'll make beautiful babies."

POPPY STOOD ON THE steps of the schoolhouse, watching as the children scattered, running off toward home, most of them needing to hurry to get chores done. It was only two weeks before school was out for the summer, and the older boys had already begun staying home so they could help in the fields.

"Miss Smith?" a voice called from behind.

Poppy turned, smiling. She'd thought he'd forgotten about her. "Mr. Alexander."

"Jacob."

"Then it's Poppy."

"Are you ready to leave?" he asked.

Poppy hurried into the schoolhouse and picked up her books and lunch pail. "I am now," she said quickly.

He took her books and lunch pail from her. "I guess I should carry Teacher's books."

Poppy laughed softly. "Just don't let the children see you. They'll have a great deal to say about it.

He chuckled. "You must not be much older than some of your students."

"I'm not," she said. "The older boys are gone until after harvest, but the older girls see me more as an equal. I went to school with most of them. It's an odd situation for certain. But I don't need everyone in town calling you Teacher's beau. That would get uncomfortable for both of us."

"Oh, I don't know. It kind of has a nice ring to it, don't you think?"

She laughed, shaking her head. "Small town gossip can take on a life of its own. I promise, we don't want to go that route."

"I wouldn't know. I was born and raised in New York City. The first time I left was when I joined the Union Army and went to Camp Curtin in Pennsylvania."

"That war seems so far away here. I mean, I know it's over now, but it never felt like it really touched us."

"It touched me," he said, frowning. "It touched me where it hurt."

Poppy felt the weight of his gaze, the sincerity in his words stirring something deep within her. "I'm sorry."

"Everybody's got a past, Poppy," he found himself saying. "I hope you have a good evening." He gave her back her books and lunch pail when they reached her door.

She watched him turn to leave, the tall grasses swaying in his wake. She hoped they had more opportunities to get to know one another.

"Good night, Miss Smith," Jacob called softly over his shoulder.

"Good night, Mr. Alexander," she replied.

JACOB ALEXANDER LEANED against the weathered wood of the Clover Creek General Store, his gaze fixed on the schoolhouse across the way where Poppy Smith was dismissing her class for the day. As the last child darted past, Jacob's eyes found Poppy again, her flaming red hair easy to spot.

"Mr. Alexander?" A voice broke through his contemplation. "You planning on standing there all day?"

Jacob offered a smile to the storekeeper who had stepped out beside him. "Just taking in the view, Mr. Jensen."

"Miss Smith is quite the view," the older man agreed before retreating inside his store.

Now, as he watched her close the schoolhouse door behind her, he felt an urge to step closer into her world. He wanted to know everything about her.

The notion that Poppy might share his curiosity gave rise to a sense of anticipation. "Miss Smith!" he called out, crossing the distance between them with a few purposeful strides.

"Mr. Alexander," Poppy greeted him, a hint of surprise etching her features as she turned to face him. Her green eyes met his with an openness that quickened his pulse.

"Forgive the intrusion, but I was hoping you might entertain a question or two about Clover Creek," he said.

"Of course," she replied, her lips curving into a soft smile. "I'd be happy to help."

"Perhaps you could show me around sometime? Introduce me?" Jacob ventured.

Poppy regarded him for a moment, her gaze searching his. "I think that can be arranged."

JACOB STOOD OUTSIDE the modest structure of the Clover Creek schoolhouse, his gaze lingering on the wooden doorway. The windows were dark now, the laughter and chatter of children long since faded into the quiet dusk.

"Building a dairy farm won't be an easy task," Charles had warned him earlier, "It's not just the land that's tough, but winning over the folk here. We're a close-knit bunch."

Jacob's thoughts turned to Poppy. In her presence, he sensed a kinship, but also the complexities of intertwining his life with someone else's.

"Mr. Alexander?"

The voice startled him from his reverie, and he turned to see Margaret Prewitt approaching. "Hope you don't mind me saying, but you've got that look about you. The same one my husband had when he first set eyes on this place."

"Is that so?" Jacob replied, attempting a smile.

"Definitely." Margaret nodded solemnly. "But remember, the land here can either break you or make you. It all depends on how much you're willing to fight for what you want."

"Thank you, Mrs. Prewitt," he said. "I'll keep that in mind."

And somewhere within him, nestled between trepidation and yearning, lay the silent prayer that Poppy Smith might just be exactly what he needed in life.

Chapter Two

Jacob paced the floorboards of his humble farmhouse. He paused before the mirror, scrutinizing the man who stared back at him with eyes the color of a stormy sky.

"Poppy," he murmured to his reflection. "I have come to like you more than I ever thought possible." He cleared his throat, trying again. "Miss Poppy, would you do me the honor—no, no."

A former Union soldier, he was no stranger to facing fearsome battles, but the prospect of asking Poppy to marry him had him shaking. His brother's memory haunted him, a silent reminder that life's moments were fleeting and precious.

The ring, a simple band of gold with an engraving of two joined hands, felt heavy in his pocket, its weight a testament to the gravity of his intentions.

MEANWHILE, THE CLOVER Creek schoolhouse buzzed with the laughter and chatter of children. Poppy stood amidst her pupils, her flaming red hair adding color to the simply decorated schoolroom.

"Settle down now, children," she said, her voice a gentle lilt that immediately drew the room into attentive silence. She moved between the desks with grace, offering a smile here, a word of encouragement there.

"Remember, patience is just like planting a seed," Poppy explained. "It needs time to grow, but with enough care and attention, it will blossom beautifully."

Her gaze settled on a small girl struggling with her letters, and Poppy knelt beside her, guiding the child's hand with tender patience.

Poppy rang the bell, signaling the end of the school day, and the children scurried out, leaving Poppy alone with her thoughts. Her gaze kept scanning for Jacob, who was usually there to walk her home. She tried not to be too disappointed, knowing the man had work to do.

Jacob walked toward the Clover Creek schoolhouse. In his pocket, he carried a small leather pouch, its contents more precious than anything he'd ever owned.

Poppy was tidying the day's lessons, her fingers brushing over the worn wooden surfaces of the desks as if imprinting upon them the knowledge they had absorbed.

"Poppy," Jacob called out softly as he stepped into the classroom.

She turned toward him, her green eyes reflecting a mix of surprise and curiosity. "Jacob," she greeted.

Jacob closed the distance between them thinking of the new life he was determined to build here in this untamed land. He stood before her now, a former Union soldier, his dark hair and eyes a stark contrast to the softness that seemed to envelop her.

"Poppy," he said again, his tone more intimate this time, "I've come to ask you something." His hand trembled slightly as he reached into his pocket and withdrew the leather pouch.

Her breath caught, and a delicate flush crept over her cheeks.

Jacob took a deep breath, steadying himself against the tide of emotions that threatened to overwhelm him. He opened the pouch and revealed a simple gold band.

"Out here, life's tough and full of uncertainty," Jacob started. "But one thing I'm certain of is how I feel about you. You've brought learning and light to this place, just like you've brought hope to my heart."

He knelt down on one knee. The humble schoolroom became a chapel of promise in that moment.

"Poppy," Jacob continued, "will you marry me? Will you share this hard but beautiful life with me?"

Tears glistened in Poppy's eyes, the weight of her own grief and struggles finding solace in the bond Jacob offered. She looked upon the man who had seen the horrors of war and emerged seeking peace, who now laid bare his heart before her. And in the quiet resolve of his gaze, she saw not only the shadows of loss but also the glimmer of a shared dream.

"Yes, Jacob," she whispered. "Yes, I will."

He slid the simple gold band onto her finger. She gazed down at her hand, turning it this way and that to catch the light streaming through the windows of the schoolhouse.

JACOB STOOD NEAR THE altar of the Clover Creek Church, his heart thrumming like a drumbeat against his ribs. Memories of loss and survival from his time as a Union soldier swirled in his mind. He could almost hear the rhythmic clop of hooves and the distant bugle calls that haunted his dreams.

"Beautiful, isn't it?" whispered his future sister-in-law, her hand resting briefly on his arm before she joined the other attendees.

"Very," Jacob murmured, though his eyes never left the entrance, awaiting Poppy.

When she finally appeared at the doorway, his heart skipped a beat. Her hair was crowned with delicate white blossoms. She stepped forward, her green eyes finding his, and the world outside faded into insignificance.

Poppy's hand found Jacob's, and he felt the tremor of his fingers as if they belonged to another man. Pastor Scott looked between them before clearing his throat. "Dearly beloved, we are gathered here today..."

Her hand was warm and comforting in his, an anchor amidst the churning sea of his emotions.

As the pastor told Jacob he may kiss the bride, the congregation erupted into applause.

It seemed the entire community was there for the wedding and reception. Everyone had brought a dish, and they all gathered together to eat the food.

The air was thick with the scent of roasted meats and freshly baked bread, blending with the sweet perfume of wildflowers that adorned the tables.

"May your love be as steadfast as the mountains," Mr. Williams said.

"And as fertile as the valleys that cradle our rivers," another added.

Though she had never enjoyed being the center of attention, Poppy was happy to be there and have her love for Jacob celebrated. Now that school was out for the summer, they would have months to get used to one another.

Poppy's fingers traced the intricate lace of her wedding dress, the fabric whispering secrets of a new life as she sought out Margaret Prewitt in the quiet solitude of the boarding house kitchen.

"Margaret?" Poppy's voice fluttered like the wings of a sparrow, uncertain yet yearning for guidance.

"Ah, my friend," Margaret said, turning from where she stood by the fireplace. Her face softened at the sight of the young bride. "Come sit with me."

"Margaret, I..." Poppy began, hesitating as she perched on a wooden stool across from the older woman. "I want to be a good wife to Jacob, to build a life as strong as the one you have carved here. But I fear I know so little about...well, about marriage."

"Dear girl," Margaret replied, taking Poppy's hands in hers, warm and steady. "There is no one way to make a marriage work. It's like tending a garden—you plant the seeds, you water them, but most importantly, you must give them time to grow."

"Time," Poppy echoed, her eyes reflecting the flicker of firelight.

"And patience," Margaret continued, releasing Poppy's hands and gesturing expressively. "You two will need to learn each other's ways. It's a dance, Poppy. You never know if you'll lead or follow."

"Communication too, I suppose?" Poppy ventured.

"Without a doubt," Margaret affirmed, nodding. "Speak your truths, Poppy, even when it's hard. Especially then. Don't let silence take root between you, lest it grows thorns."

"And compromise?"

"Ah," Margaret laughed softly. "Compromise is the very soil of marriage. You give a little, he gives a little, and in the middle, you find happiness. It was that way with my first husband, and even more so with Jamie. He loves the girls from my first marriage, and he also loves his own children dearly. But the answer is always meeting in the middle."

"Thank you, Margaret," Poppy said. "I will do all I can to be an obedient wife. I'm not sure I have it in me, but I will try."

"Remember this," Margaret added. "Love is a choice you make every day, not just when the trail is easy and the sun is shining. It's choosing each other, again and again, even when the storms come."

"I will remember," Poppy promised. She would choose Jacob, choose love, each day, no matter what life might throw their way.

JACOB STOOD AT THE threshold of his small farmhouse, his dark eyes taking in the simple furnishings that he had arranged with care.

Poppy's presence behind him, her hand light on his arm, was a warm reminder that he was here, now, on the cusp of a new beginning. Her touch seemed to steady the tremors of the past that threatened to rise within him. Turning to face her, Jacob saw the flicker of anticipation in her eyes.

"Jacob," she whispered, a gentle entreaty laced with the strength that had first drawn him to her.

He could only nod, his voice momentarily lost as he reached out to lightly caress a stray curl that had escaped.

The cabin seemed to hold its breath as Jacob took Poppy's hand and led her to the edge of the bed, the quilt beneath them a patchwork of community and care. They sat side by side.

"Are you nervous?" Jacob asked.

"Jacob Alexander," Poppy said with quiet conviction, her green eyes meeting his steadily. "There is no place I would rather be than here, with you."

He leaned forward, capturing her lips in a kiss. As they slowly laid down, hands exploring with a surprising tenderness, a sigh escaped Poppy. It was a sound that seemed to carry away the remnants of apprehension, leaving only the profound intimacy of two souls embarking on life's journey together.

The night unfolded with a rhythm as old as time. And in the quiet after, with Poppy's head resting against his chest, Jacob allowed himself to truly believe— perhaps for the first time since his brother had fallen in battle—he had found a place to call home.

POPPY STOOD IN THE heart of their farmhouse kitchen, her red hair pinned back neatly as she stirred a pot of stew. The aroma of herbs and tender meat filled the air, a scent that promised warmth and comfort. She had embraced her new role with enthusiasm. Every corner of the home bloomed with her touch, from the freshly laundered curtains to the wildflowers gracing the table.

"Jacob will love this," she murmured to herself. She glanced out the window. Any moment now, he would return from the fields, and they would sit together, enjoying one another's company.

But Jacob did not come. Poppy served herself a bowl of stew, eating alone at the wooden table set for two. The chair across from her remained empty.

Later, Jacob finally appeared. He moved with a weariness that seemed to weigh upon his shoulders, a silent testament to the heavy load he carried within.

"Evening, Poppy," he said.

"Evening," she replied, rising to greet him. "Dinner's ready. It's still warm."

"Thank you," he nodded focusing on the bowl she placed before him. He ate with an absent-mindedness that she'd never seen.

She watched him, worrying. Since their vows were exchanged beneath the small church's wooden beams, she had witnessed the growing chasms of silence between them.

Each day, Jacob's distance seemed to widen. His brother's loss at war was a wound that time had yet to heal, and it kept him tethered to yesteryears, even as Poppy reached for a future together. She wished she knew the right words to say to soothe him, but she had no idea what would make him feel better.

"Are you all right?" she finally asked. She kept her voice soft, but she wanted to jump up and yell at him to talk to her.

He looked up, his dark eyes meeting hers briefly before finding refuge in the depths of his stew. "I'm fine."

"Jacob—" she started, but he stood abruptly, pushing the chair back with a scrape that echoed too loudly in the quiet room.

"Need to check on the cows one last time before bed," he said, and without waiting for a response, he was gone.

Poppy sat there, surrounded by the life they had built, and felt an aching solitude. With a sigh, she cleared the table, her mind replaying

Margaret's advice. Communication, compromise, patience; she clung to these words like lifelines.

Yet as she washed the dishes, Poppy realized that choosing love was more than just a daily decision. It was an act of courage. Even as she wished she knew how to close the gap between them, she realized that Jacob would have to let go of his past before that could happen.

As she prepared for bed, folding the quilt back with care, Poppy allowed herself a moment to imagine a future where the walls echoed with the sounds of joy, not just the creaks of solitude. She wanted what her siblings had found.

THE WIND HOWLED OUTSIDE the wooden confines of their farmhouse. Poppy sat by the hearth. The fire's warmth was a stark contrast to the cold that had crept into her bones. She wished she could find a way to get Jacob to communicate with her, but with every day, she felt as if she loved him more, and it seemed he slipped further away.

In the dim light, her hands moved methodically, mending a tear in one of Jacob's shirts. The thread looped over and under, a whisper-soft sound amidst the creaking of the homestead that surrounded them.

"Life wasn't supposed to be this lonesome," she murmured. Her red hair, usually so fiery and vibrant, lay limp across her shoulders, echoing her weary spirit. She said her tenth prayer of the day, begging her Heavenly Father to help Jacob confide in her.

There was no reply, no comforting embrace—just the endless wind and the memory of Jacob's dark eyes avoiding hers. The brother he'd lost on the battlefield haunted more than just his dreams. It seemed to prevent him from being able to warm up to Poppy as his wife.

Poppy knew that whatever may come, she would stand by Jacob's side, enduring the hardships, sharing in the triumphs, and weathering each storm together.

"Love is a journey," she whispered into the silence. "And we've only just begun."

As Poppy slipped beneath the quilt, she held tightly to that sliver of hope. In the quiet moments before sleep claimed her, she envisioned a time when laughter would replace the somber tones that now resonated through their home. A time when Jacob's touch would convey love.

Chapter Three

Poppy tied her apron. The kitchen of their small homestead was warm, a haven from the crisp morning air that swept across the Oregon plains. With practiced hands, she sifted through the flour, fingers grazing the coarse grains as she prepared to knead the dough for bread. She had learned to bake it just how Jacob preferred, with a touch of honey and a crust baked to golden perfection.

Every corner of the house bore evidence of Poppy's meticulous care. Handmade curtains fluttered gently at the open windows, the floors were swept clean of the ever-encroaching dust, and wildflowers adorned the simple wooden table she recognized as Elmer's work.

As the bread baked, releasing a comforting aroma into the room, Poppy set about preparing a hearty breakfast. She fried bacon until it sizzled and popped alongside eggs from their hens, which she cooked just shy of runny—just the way he might have liked them if he ever voiced a preference. She could remember her mother telling Sarah that the way to a man's heart was through his stomach. She only wished Jacob had heard the same thing.

"Breakfast is ready," she said softly, as Jacob finally stood and dressed.

"Thank you, Poppy," Jacob murmured, taking a seat at the head of the table. His words were polite. He began to eat with mechanical precision, each bite a function of survival rather than enjoyment.

Poppy watched him from across the table, her appetite waning in the face of his detachment. She longed to reach out, to bridge the chasm with gentle words or a tender touch, but his face spoke clearly that her touch wouldn't be welcome.

"Is the bread to your liking?" she asked, hoping that he would open up and talk to her. Any conversation was better than no conversation.

"It's fine," Jacob replied without looking up.

Poppy pressed her lips together, biting back the sigh that threatened to escape. The constant longing for his affection gnawed at her insides. She knew of his past, of the brother lost on battlefields steeped in blood and sorrow. She understood that grief could be a land with no clear path forward. But she couldn't understand why he wouldn't let her soothe him.

"Jacob," she began, hesitating as she sought the courage to voice her feelings, "I wish we could... talk more. About anything, really."

He paused, his fork mid-air, and for a fleeting moment, Poppy thought she saw a flicker of something more behind the guarded veil of his eyes. But just as quickly as it appeared, it vanished.

"Maybe later, Poppy," he said quietly.

The late afternoon sun cast long shadows across the prairie as Poppy stood at the wooden gate, her fingers curled around the weathered post. She watched Sarah and Elmer's wagon approach.

"Evening, Poppy," Elmer called out, touching the brim of his hat with a calloused hand as he brought the horses to a halt. Sarah's warm smile appeared over the edge of the wagon.

"Hello, sister," Sarah greeted, her eyes soft with concern as she took in Poppy's troubled expression.

"Mind if I take a moment?" Poppy asked, her voice barely above a whisper, betraying the turmoil within.

"Of course not, dear," Sarah replied, reaching out her hand to help Poppy into the wagon.

They settled beneath the shade of an old cottonwood tree, where Hannah Scott had already spread a quilt for their gathering. The pastor's wife looked up from her mending, her eyes gentle but perceptive.

"Poppy," Hannah said, setting aside her work. "You look like you're carrying the weight of the world."

"Feels like it, sometimes," Poppy admitted, tucking a loose strand of red hair behind her ear.

"Jacob isn't giving you any trouble, is he?" Elmer's protective tone was softened by his underlying worry.

"It's not trouble, exactly..." Poppy hesitated, looking down at her hands folded in her lap. "He's just...so far away, even when he's right beside me. I cook his favorite meals, keep the house just so, but it's like he's still out there on the trail, fighting ghosts I can't see."

Hannah reached out, placing her hand over Poppy's. "I remember feeling much the same about Jed when we first married. He was a good man, but love wasn't what brought us together."

"Then how did you manage?" Poppy asked, her green eyes searching Hannah's face for some secret way to Jacob's heart.

"Time and patience," Hannah said softly. "And prayer, lots of prayer. But one day, I realized I couldn't imagine my life without him. The love came quietly, not with grand gestures or passionate declarations, but in the small moments—the shared glances, the unspoken understanding, the quiet strength we drew from each other."

"Does it ever get easier?" Poppy's voice trembled as she spoke.

"Love is like growing a garden," Sarah chimed in. "You tend to it every day, even when the soil's stubborn and the wind's relentless. And in time, it gives back more than you put in."

"Perhaps," Poppy murmured. "Perhaps it's time for me to learn the language of patience." Poppy had once had a student who didn't seem able to learn to read. But she worked with them every day until he was one of the best readers in the class. She couldn't help but wonder what that kind of patience would do for love.

"Poppy," Sarah's voice broke through the twilight hush. "Are you coming? Supper won't eat itself."

"Coming," Poppy replied.

Inside, the scent of stew mingled with the aroma of fresh bread. Jacob sat at the head of the table. Hannah's gentle smile greeted her as Poppy took her seat, the warmth in the room offering a contrast to the chill settling outside.

"Your dedication, it's something to admire," Elmer said, nodding toward Poppy with a smile that crinkled the corners of his eyes. "Jacob's a lucky man."

"Thank you, Elmer. I do try," Poppy said, her fingers fiddling with the hem of her apron.

"The effort shows," Sarah added. "You've made a wonderful home here. It's more than just cooking and cleaning—it's love stitched into every corner."

"Love is an investment," Hannah interjected. "Like the good book says, 'Love is patient, love is kind.' There's truth in waiting, in kindness—even when it feels like you're waiting for rain in a drought."

"Patience is a language I'm still learning," Poppy admitted. "But I believe in its power. I'll continue to speak it, hoping one day he'll understand."

"Jacob will come around," Elmer reassured. "It'll take time to find his way back to softer feelings."

"Still, sometimes I fear..." Poppy trailed off.

"Poppy," Sarah reached across the table, her hand resting atop hers. "Remember why you started this journey. You wanted to build something lasting."

"She's right," Hannah agreed, her eyes holding a spark that mirrored the firelight. "The heart has its own journey. Yours and Jacob's may take longer roads, but they are headed to the same destination."

"Then I shall walk that road, however long it may be," Poppy resolved, her voice steadier now. "I'll be as patient as I can. Of course, if he doesn't start talking to me a bit more, he may have to deal with my redheaded temper. I'm not sure he'd find that altogether pleasant."

They ate in companionable silence, each lost in their thoughts yet bound together by the common threads of hope and perseverance.

POPPY STOOD BY THE window, her fingers tracing the delicate lace curtains she had sewn herself. Her red hair was gathered in a loose braid, a few strands escaping to frame her thoughtful face. She gazed out at the expanse of land that stretched beyond their property.

"Jacob," she whispered to the empty room, "I wish you'd let me in."

Outside, Jacob was tending to the dairy cows, his movements deliberate and steady. The cows milled about, their lowing a familiar backdrop to his thoughts. As he leaned against the fence, his gaze settled on the rolling hills.

"Am I a coward?" he mused silently. "Or am I sparing her the burden of my broken pieces?"

The wooden boards of the porch creaked as Poppy stepped outside, her presence a silent beacon of warmth and resilience. She approached him tentatively, searching for the connection she so desperately craved.

"Jacob, supper will be ready soon," she said, her voice soft but laced with unspoken yearning. "I've made your favorite—beef stew with dumplings."

"Thank you, Poppy," he replied, the corners of his mouth lifting in a fleeting attempt at a smile. "Sounds good."

Inside the barn, Jacob grappled with the pain of his past. He remembered the brother he had lost, the blood-soaked fields, the screams that still haunted his dreams. He wanted to tell Poppy, to share the crushing weight of guilt and grief, but fear held his tongue. Each time he neared the precipice of vulnerability, the specter of his brother's accusing eyes pulled him back.

"Poppy deserves better than a shadow of a man," he thought. "What would she think of me if she knew I'd killed my own brother?"

"JACOB," POPPY CALLED out, her voice steady despite the fluttering in her chest. "Supper's ready."

He didn't turn at first, the hammer pounding loudly.

"Jacob!" she tried again.

Finally, he paused, setting the hammer down and wiping his brow with the back of his hand. His dark eyes met hers across the distance.

"Coming," he replied.

"Thank you for fixing the fence today," she said, attempting to initiate some form of conversation.

"Needed doing," was all Jacob muttered, his gaze fixed on the bowl before him.

"Jacob..." she said, "we need to talk. This—us—it can't go on like this."

He looked up then, his features hardening slightly, the lines around his eyes deepening. "What's there to talk about? I'm here. I'm fulfilling my duties as a husband."

"Being here isn't the same as being present," she retorted. "I feel like I'm living with a ghost sometimes."

"Maybe that's all I am now," he shot back. "Ghosts of men lost, dreams buried—they don't just vanish because the war ended."

"Then let me in, Jacob. Let me share the burden," Poppy pleaded, reaching a tentative hand across the table.

Jacob recoiled slightly before catching himself. He looked at her hand, then slowly placed his own atop it. It was a small gesture, far from the connection Poppy craved, but it was a start, a momentary bridge across the chasm.

The weeks turned into months. Poppy tended to the garden, the vibrant blooms juxtaposing the muted tones of their interactions. Jacob continued his labor, doing all he could to build the farm into something they could be proud of.

In the quiet moments, when the moon hung low and the coyotes howled in the distance, Poppy would lie awake, listening to Jacob's breathing. And for just a while, as sleep claimed her and the barriers of daylight faded, she allowed herself to believe their love could yet grow strong enough to withstand the trials of the trail and the echoes of war that still lingered in the air.

POPPY STOOD BY THE kitchen window. She kneaded dough with practiced hands, each push and fold a rhythmic testament to her dedication. The scent of baked bread soon filled the small cabin, weaving an unspoken invitation to warmth in a space that often felt too quiet.

Outside, Jacob tended to the dairy cows, his silhouette a steady fixture against the horizon. Though he remained distant, she found solace in the assurance that, despite the emotional void between them, he was always there.

"I talked to Mrs. Mitchell today," she said softly.

"What about?" he asked, not truly interested, but he knew the part he was supposed to play.

"I haven't been feeling well, and I talked to her about it. She thinks I'm expecting. I'm going to see the doctor tomorrow to make sure."

For once, Jacob had a reaction, and it warmed Poppy's heart. "Really? A baby?"

"Would that make you happy?" she asked.

"I honestly can't think of anything that would make me happier."

She smiled. "I hope Mrs. Mitchell is right then. I'd love to see you happy." Because she realized she never had. Whatever he was hiding was keeping him from being able to smile.

For the rest of the evening, he seemed to truly care about her. She knew he was focused on the baby, but hopefully loving the baby would translate into loving its mother. Maybe she wouldn't feel so alone any longer.

Later, Poppy climbed into bed beside her husband. Even as he slept, turned away, she reached out to lightly touch his arm, feeling the warmth of his skin beneath her fingertips.

"Goodnight, Jacob," she murmured, letting her hand rest there but a moment longer before withdrawing. "We have tomorrow, and I will not give up on us."

Chapter Four

Jacob was leaning on the fence when he heard the crunch of gravel underfoot. He turned to see Poppy, her face aglow with a mix of excitement and trepidation. Her shadow stretched long across the ground, reaching for him like an omen.

"Jacob," she called, her voice quivering slightly with the weight of her news.

He straightened up and met her halfway, noting the flush in her cheeks that wasn't there from just the walk home. "What is it, Poppy?" he asked, his heart starting to beat a little faster. Maybe it was the way she held herself, or the almost imperceptible tremor in her smile, but something significant hovered between them.

"I've just come back from Dr. Bentley's office," she said, her hands intertwining nervously before her. "And...we're going to have a baby."

For a moment, everything stopped—the wind, the rustling leaves, the distant mooing of cattle. Jacob felt a surge of emotion he hadn't experienced since before the war had taken his brother. It was as if Poppy's words had unlocked something deep within him.

"Truly?" His voice was barely a whisper, laden with a hope he'd dared not entertain.

"Truly," she confirmed, her voice lifting in joy.

With a sudden burst of energy, he closed the remaining distance and swept Poppy into his arms, spinning her around as laughter bubbled from them both. He held her tight, his dark eyes shining with unshed tears of happiness, and whispered promises into her hair. "If it's a boy, I want to name him Lucas. After my brother."

Poppy nodded. "Lucas is a fine name. I like it."

The following week, Jacob threw himself into his work with renewed vigor, fixing fences with a whistle on his lips and waking before dawn to tend to the milking. Poppy watched him with a warmth in her chest, her hand often resting on her still-flat belly, dreaming of the family they were about to become.

But as quickly as this newfound joy had come, it was gone. The shadows in Jacob's eyes returned, deeper and more haunted than before. He started to retreat again into the silence that had so often enveloped him. It settled over the farm like a thick fog.

Poppy noticed the change one evening when Jacob came in from the barn later than usual, his supper cold and untouched on the table. She watched him from the doorway, the lines of his face etched with a sorrow that seemed to have no end.

"Jacob?" she ventured softly, the concern clear in her voice.

He looked up, his gaze distant, as if he were seeing through her to a place she couldn't follow. "I'm tired, Poppy," he said, his voice hollow. "Just tired."

Poppy felt a chill run down her spine. The word 'tired' hung in the air, but she knew it wasn't a truthful comment. No, it was more than being tired. And once again, she was no part of it.

POPPY'S FINGERS TREMBLED as she folded the last of the schoolchildren's drawings, her heart heavy. Her mind was not on the sketches of wildflowers and prairie dogs but on Jacob, his recent joy at her pregnancy now a fleeting memory. She brushed a stray lock of fiery hair from her face and made a decision.

As Poppy entered their homestead, the creaking of the wooden floor under her boots echoed in the sparse room, mirroring the tension that hung in the air. Jacob sat by the hearth staring into the flames as if they held answers to questions she hadn't yet asked.

"Jacob," Poppy began, her voice steady despite the quiver of uncertainty within her, "we need to talk."

He glanced up, dark eyes meeting hers for just a moment before he looked away. "Everything's fine, Poppy," he murmured.

"Fine?" she pressed, stepping closer, her skirts whispering against the wooden planks. "You've been as distant as the horizon since...since we learned of the baby." She paused, watching his jaw tighten. "Is there something on your mind? Something you're not telling me?"

Jacob stood abruptly, his chair scraping back with a jarring sound. "I've work to do," he said.

"Work can wait!" Poppy's voice rose, filled with an anger she could no longer contain. She reached out, grasping his arm. "Jacob, look at me!"

He turned to her then. "Poppy, please," he said softly.

"Please, what? Please pretend that everything is as it should be?" She searched his face. "Jacob," she insisted, her resolve hardening, "if there is anything between us, let it be honesty. I beg of you."

Finally, Jacob exhaled, a slow surrender escaping his lips. "I married you so I could carry on my family name. I had no one in the world, and now, I have a child coming," he confessed. "Love had nothing to do with it."

Poppy felt the room tilt, the foundation of their life together cracking beneath her feet. She released his arm, stepping back as if distance could shield her from him.

"I see," she said softly. Keeping her voice low took every bit of effort that she had inside her. She wanted to take her skillet and clobber him over the head with it. Or take her broom and shove it all the way up his nose until it came poking out of the top of his head.

"Poppy, I..." Jacob began.

She looked at him then, really looked, seeing past the mask to the grieving man inside him. "Thank you for your honesty, Jacob," she managed. "At least now I know where we stand."

With that, Poppy turned away from him, her steps measured and deliberate as she retreated to the sanctuary of the kitchen, not caring where he was or what he was doing. He didn't love her. What else did she need to know?

Poppy slipped through the door, the latch clicking softly behind her. It was windy with a chill that seeped through her shawl, every gust of wind a welcome companion. If she focused on the cold, she wouldn't focus on what an idiot she'd been to marry Jacob. She had envisioned love, companionship, children playing in the yard—but these were fantasies.

With each step along the dirt path that wound its way through Clover Creek, Poppy's thoughts wandered to the marriage she wanted. One filled with love and tender moments. Not just with duty and growing a family. How could she have been so stupid?

She stopped by the brook that meandered past their homestead, its waters gurgling over rocks and roots, indifferent to human sorrow. She'd once thought they would have picnics by the stream while their children played. But her illusions were gone as sure as her heart was broken.

"Love," she murmured to the uncaring stream, "where art thou?"

The whisper of her voice seemed to mock her. Now, the future loomed before her, bleak and barren.

Yet even as despair clutched at her skirts, a defiant spark kindled within her. Was it not better to know the truth? To face the world with eyes wide open, no matter how hard it was?

"Perhaps," Poppy conceded, "but oh, to be cherished."

Of course, what she wanted mattered little. Jacob didn't love her, and she couldn't force him to try.

"Jacob!" There was no response.

"Jacob," she whispered to herself this time.

With each passing day, Jacob seemed to delve deeper into his work, the farm becoming both his sanctuary and prison. He would return late after Poppy had taken her solitary supper.

And so, the days stretched into weeks, marked by the relentless cycle of dawn to dusk. Poppy busied herself with the small tasks that made up life on the frontier but found little solace in them. The farm, once a shared dream, now felt like a barren landscape mirroring her empty heart.

Finally, she'd had enough of his nonsense. If he didn't come when she called him for supper, then he didn't need to eat. She wasn't going to keep his food warm for him or go out to try to find him anymore. He would treat her with the respect his wife deserved—whether he loved her or not—or he could go hungry.

"Poppy?" The sound of her name startled her, and she turned to see Jacob standing at the edge of the field, his expression unreadable.

"Supper's ready," she said.

"Thank you," he replied and turned back toward the barn without another glance.

Without even looking at him again, she dumped his supper into the yard and ate her supper. She wasn't going to play his game any longer.

POPPY WALKED INTO TOWN and bought some wheat the following day, not letting Jacob know because she was certain he didn't care. When she reached the homestead, she paused, her hand hovering over the doorknob. A part of her wished to find Jacob inside, ready to greet her with an embrace. But there was no one home. No one but Poppy.

Poppy walked into the kitchen to make supper. She knew she would probably throw Jacob's half out, but she still cooked for him. It didn't seem to matter how he felt about her. She still loved him.

"Is there any hope for us?" she whispered to the empty room.

Jacob's chair across from hers remained unoccupied, the indentation on its cushion slowly fading.

Poppy pressed her hand against the cool glass of the window, watching for a sign of Jacob returning from the fields or the barn.

POPPY HEARD THE FAMILIAR creak of the homestead's gate. She glanced up from her lonely vigil at the window to see Sarah, her sister, making her way up the path, a basket of fresh bread and preserves swinging in her hand.

"Sarah," Poppy greeted. The comfort of family was a balm even on the raw edges of her heartache.

"Poppy," Sarah said with a concerned furrow between her brows, stepping into the dimming kitchen. "I brought some apricot preserves; I remember they're your favorite."

"Thank you," Poppy murmured. She knew she was losing weight that she couldn't afford to lose while she carried the baby, but she didn't know how to stop it. The preserves reminded her of brighter days, of laughter shared over breakfast that now seemed an age away.

"Poppy?" Sarah's gentle hand touched her arm, urging her to sit beside her at the wooden table. "What weighs on you? You know you can tell me anything."

The floodgates opened, and words poured out of Poppy. "It's Jacob...He's never here, and when he is, it's like he's miles away. I feel so alone, Sarah. I feel abandoned."

Sarah listened without interruption, her presence a steady rock amidst the whirlpool of Poppy's emotions. When the last sob had left her sister's lips, she spoke softly, "Poppy, love isn't always lightning and thunder. Sometimes it's the quiet growth after a long winter. It blooms with time and patience."

Poppy nodded. "When we first found out that I was expecting, everything changed for a little while, but now he's back to not remembering I'm here."

As the sisters' conversation waned, a gentle knock at the door interrupted their communion. Hannah Scott stood there, her own face etched with lines of empathy and understanding.

"May I come in?" she asked. Within moments, the pastor's wife was seated at the table, her hands enveloping Poppy's.

"Poppy, I've seen the strain between you and Jacob," Hannah began, her eyes reflecting the setting sun's fading light. "Jed and I, we've weathered our own storms. There were days I thought the love we had was lost in the wilderness of our struggles."

"How did you find your way back?" Poppy asked, her voice barely above a whisper, seeking the secret map Hannah had used to navigate her marital trials.

"It takes time," Hannah replied, "and faith—not just in each other, but in the journey you've undertaken together. Love is a commitment that endures beyond affection. It's a choice to walk side by side."

POPPY WANDERED TO THE edge of the wheat field. The Clover Creek schoolhouse, where she had taught, stood in the distance, its windows reflecting the late afternoon sun—a beacon of routine and escape from her private turmoil.

As she stood there, she made a decision that would change the course of her life no matter how it went. She would move back in with Sarah and see how long it took Jacob to realize she was gone.

The wind picked up, sending a chill through her bones and teasing her flaming red hair into wild disarray. She wrapped her arms around herself, not just for warmth, but in an attempt to hold together the fragments of her resolve. Could she leave? Did she have the courage to leave a man who didn't love her and never had? Or would she crumble as soon as someone from town looked at her?

"Perhaps..." Poppy murmured. Her heart ached at the thought of abandoning the promise she had made before God and their small community. Leaving Jacob would mean turning her back on the vows she had taken so seriously, yet his absence was like a drought upon her soul, draining her of joy.

As the sun dipped lower, casting long shadows across the land, Poppy's inner tempest quieted. A moment of clarity emerged, as clear and sharp as the horizon line that severed earth from heaven. She remembered their shared laughter, the way he had looked at her when they first met, full of a different kind of longing.

As hard as it was to leave him, she knew she had to do it. She needed to leave for herself. Because being unloved and unwanted wasn't something she enjoyed.

With a newfound determination, Poppy turned back toward the house they shared. She would pack her things and go spend some time with her sister and her family. Sarah had let her know she was always welcome, and she was ready to find out if her sister meant it or if she was just saying it to be kind.

Chapter Five

Poppy stood in the doorway of the small cabin she shared with Jacob, her eyes tracing over the life they had hastily built together. With each item she placed into her worn-out satchel—a few dresses, her mother's locket, the quilt Sarah had made for her when she first started teaching—she felt pieces of her heart splinter.

Poppy heaved the last of her belongings onto the wagon. Her flaming red hair lay damp against her forehead from exertion. She took a moment to glance back at the home she was leaving behind, letting herself feel the pang of loss for what could have been.

"Come on, Poppy," Sarah called gently from the driver's bench. "Let's head home."

With a deep breath, Poppy climbed beside her sister, the wagon creaking under the shift of weight as they set off toward the King family homestead.

Two days passed, filled with the quiet company of Sarah and the mundane tasks that kept Poppy's hands busy and her mind numb. She found solace in the rhythm of kneading dough and the simplicity of hanging laundry on the line.

She was even pleased not to have to make decisions about what to cook every day. It seemed to her that eating three times a day was a waste. Of course, the child within her demanded food to grow.

On the third morning, as Poppy bent over the garden pulling weeds, the sound of hoofbeats disturbed the stillness. She straightened, brushing dirt from her hands as she watched a familiar figure dismount from his horse. Jacob's dark hair was tousled by the wind, and his eyes, which once seemed to hold the depth of night, now appeared clouded with confusion.

"Jacob," she greeted him coolly, her arms crossing over her chest in a protective shield.

"Poppy," he replied.

"Did it really take you two full days to notice I was gone?" Poppy couldn't keep the bitterness from her voice, her green eyes flashing with the accusation. She'd never understood the phrase that love and hate were opposite sides of the same coin before. As much as she loved Jacob, he could make her angrier than anyone else on earth.

Jacob's jaw tightened, a muscle ticking in his cheek. He looked around the yard, taking in the absence of her presence in their shared space.

"Poppy, I—" He began, but she cut him off with a sharp wave of her hand.

"Save your words, Jacob. I've heard them all before." Her voice was as somber as the twilight descending upon the landscape, and she turned away.

"Poppy," Jacob said, "I've been...preoccupied. But you can't think I wouldn't notice your absence. The silence in the house was deafening without you."

"The silence in the house is deafening even if I'm there! I talk to myself, but I don't answer. And it's not as if you want to talk to me. You've proven that time and again."

"I miss your voice."

"Silence can be a comfort to some," she said, not turning to face him. "Perhaps you're just not used to it yet."

Jacob took a step closer, and she could feel the warmth of him just out of reach. Poppy understood loss. It was a language they both spoke too fluently. But where Jacob had let it define him, Poppy fought with every breath to love despite it.

"Poppy," he tried again, his tone softer this time, "I didn't mean for things to become...what they are."

She finally turned to look at him, seeing the way the last light of day played across his troubled features. It would have been so easy to melt into his apology. But the trail of their love was fraught with the ruts of his indifference, and Poppy knew she needed to heal before she could return to him if she ever could.

"Maybe not, Jacob," she acknowledged. "But it doesn't change that they did. And it doesn't change that I'm here now, with Sarah, where I should have been all along."

He looked as if he wanted to say more, to bridge the gap between them with words or perhaps an embrace. But the set of Poppy's shoulders told him all he needed to know. It was going to take a lot more than one quick conversation to get her to return home.

"Take care of yourself, Poppy," he said finally, sounding utterly defeated. "And take care of my baby."

"I always do," she replied as she walked away, leaving Jacob standing alone with the realization that her absence was a void nothing but her presence could fill.

JACOB STOOD ON THE porch of Sarah's modest homestead. The door swung open with a creak, and there she was—Poppy.

"Poppy," he began, his voice rough. "You need to come home."

Her green eyes flashed. "Home?" she asked. "Your house never felt like home, Jacob. It took me leaving for you to even notice my absence!"

"Poppy, I—" His words faltered under her glare.

"Two days, Jacob. Two days before you came looking." She crossed her arms, her stance as rigid as the beliefs that rooted her.

"Please, just come back, we can—"

"Can what? Continue living as strangers under the same roof?" Her voice rose, and the air between them crackled with the tension of unspoken grievances.

"Dammit, Poppy, I'm trying here!" He stepped forward, closing the distance between them, but she was immovable.

"Try harder!" And with a swift movement, her hand reached down and picked up her shoe from beside the door. In one fluid motion, it sailed through the air, narrowly missing his head as he ducked.

"Goodness, woman!" he exclaimed, part shock, part admiration coloring his tone.

"Get out of here, Jacob. I won't be coming back to a loveless marriage," she spat.

He picked up the discarded shoe, turning it over in his hands. "I'll leave," he said quietly, "but this isn't over."

"Isn't it?" Her voice was softer now, but the resolve remained.

"Poppy, I—" He stopped, realizing any further words were futile. With a heavy heart, he mounted his horse, still clutching her shoe.

As he rode home, he felt a stirring deep within—a quickening of his spirit he hadn't felt in years. It surged through him—the realization that it was Poppy who made him feel alive.

An image of her anger imprinted itself upon his mind. Her strength and that redheaded temper—it awakened something within him.

The war had stripped him of much, taught him about survival with loss and grief. But Poppy...she was teaching him about responsibility—not just to the land or the cattle, but to the heart.

JACOB HITCHED THE CHESTNUT mare to the buggy with meticulous care. "Today," he murmured to himself. Today, he would start over with Poppy.

The drive to Sarah's house was a slow one, deliberately so. Jacob took the long way around, letting the gentle sway of the buggy lull him into a state of reflection. When he finally arrived, he found Poppy sitting on the porch, wrapped in a shawl against the morning chill.

"Morning, Poppy," he greeted her, the words careful, respectful. His dark eyes met hers, searching for a sign of forgiveness.

"Jacob," she replied, her tone guarded yet not unkind. She descended the steps, eyeing the buggy with a mix of curiosity and caution.

"Would you join me for a drive?" he asked, extending a hand to help her up. It was a simple gesture, but one loaded with significance. Her fingers were cool as they brushed his, a fleeting touch that sent a jolt through him.

They drove in silence at first. Jacob stole glances at Poppy, wishing she'd say something. Anything. He had no idea how she was feeling, but he was pleased she'd joined him. He reached out and took her hand, feeling the roughness of her skin from days of hard work. She didn't pull away.

"Poppy, I..." He faltered, the weight of his words heavy on his tongue. "I've missed this. Missed you."

She looked at him then. "Jacob, why now? Why all of this?"

"Because I've been a fool," he admitted. "And because I can't imagine my life without you in it."

"Do you only want me because of the baby?" she asked, wishing she could keep the sadness from her voice.

"The baby isn't real to me yet. It's an idea. You are real to me. The softness of your skin, the sound of your voice. It's you I miss, Poppy, not the child you carry."

Poppy watched him for a moment, wondering if he was telling the truth. She felt obligated to give him another chance because of the vows they'd made and the child she was expecting. And for her heart. But would he just break it again?

SUNDAY CAME, AND WITH it the church service that gathered the whole community together. Jacob stood at the entrance, scanning the crowd until he found Poppy. He approached her, wanting to be close to her if only for the time they were in the church.

"May I sit with you?" he asked, his voice barely above a whisper.

"All right," she consented, moving over to make space for him on the pew.

The sermon spoke of redemption and sacrifice, themes that resonated deep within Jacob's battered soul. As the preacher's words filled the small wooden chapel, Jacob felt a renewed sense of purpose—to be a better man, for Poppy and for their unborn child.

When the service ended, he offered his arm, and she took it. They walked out together, stepping into the sunlight that bathed everything in a hopeful glow. Without a word, he led her to the buggy, and they embarked on another drive—a silent promise hanging between them.

"Please come home, Poppy," Jacob said after a long stretch of silence. "I know I've got no right to ask, after all I've done, but I'm begging you. I feel so lost without you."

Poppy turned to look at him, her expression unreadable. Jacob laid bare his heart, vulnerable and exposed, waiting for her verdict.

POPPY STOOD IN THE center of Sarah's parlor, her fingers idly tracing the outline of her swollen belly. The room was dim, dust motes dancing in the slivers of light that managed to pry through the closed drapes. She could hear Jacob outside.

"Are you sure about this, Poppy?" Sarah asked, her voice laced with concern.

"Things will be different," Poppy murmured more to herself than to Sarah. "He said they would be."

Sarah's brow furrowed, and she reached out, placing a gentle hand on Poppy's arm. "You know I'm here, no matter what, right?"

Poppy nodded, a lump forming in her throat. She didn't feel like she had much choice—she was four months along, and the baby needed a father. A proper family. "I know, Sarah. Thank you."

They moved methodically through the house, gathering the few belongings Poppy had brought with her when she sought refuge with Sarah. Her hands trembled as she folded clothes.

"You two better stay for supper," Sarah insisted when they had collected everything. Her tone left no room for argument.

"Supper sounds good," Jacob said from the doorway. His eyes met Poppy's, searching, seeking forgiveness or perhaps reassurance.

"Thank you, Sarah," Poppy replied, forcing a smile. It was a simple gesture, a meal among family, but it felt like a farewell—a subtle acknowledgment of the threshold she was about to cross back into a world where uncertainty ruled.

They sat around Sarah's humble table, the spread simple but hearty. Beans stewed with salt pork, cornbread baked to a golden hue, and apple preserves—all laid out on plates that had seen better days.

"Remember, things have got to change," Poppy said quietly as she pushed a spoonful of beans around her plate.

"They will," he promised. Poppy hoped that this time, the promise would hold, would take root like the seeds Sarah planted each spring, and bloom into something new, something better.

The meal ended, and they lingered for a while, not quite ready to step out into the fading light, to face the journey back to what once was home.

The wagon wheels rolled over the uneven path, a rhythmic thrumming that seemed to echo Poppy's heartbeat. It was dark, and the only light came from the lantern on the buggy itself.

Poppy sat beside him, wrapped in a quilt she had brought from Sarah's, and she shivered, not entirely from the cold. The silence between them stretched out until Jacob reached over and took one of her hands.

"Poppy," he said softly. It was the first word he'd spoken since they left Sarah's house.

She turned to look at him, her eyes searching his face in the dim light. And then, without a word, he leaned in, his lips finding hers in a kiss that was at once familiar and startlingly new. It was a kiss that spoke of regret and longing.

In the confines of their small cabin, they rediscovered each other. Clothes were shed, and they came together with a tenderness that seemed both out of place and natural at the same time. That night, under the heavy blanket of darkness, they made love with a gentle urgency.

Poppy was the first to stir the following morning. She rose quietly, careful not to wake Jacob, who lay beside her, his breaths deep and even in sleep.

She dressed in silence and tiptoed to the small stove, stoking the embers to life before setting a pot of water to boil. There were eggs to be gathered from the hens out back, and she retrieved them with a practiced hand. Breakfast would be simple: eggs, whatever bread was left, and tea. As she cracked the shells against the rim of the skillet, she allowed herself to feel a cautious spark of hope. Maybe, just maybe, things really could be different this time.

Jacob stirred as the scent of cooking food filled the cabin, and he joined her at the table, his hair tousled from sleep. They ate mostly in silence. Poppy sipped her tea, its warmth spreading through her, and allowed herself to believe, if only for this fleeting moment, that they may be able to make things work between them.

THE MORNING AIR HELD a chill that whispered of the changing seasons, and Poppy wrapped her shawl tighter around her shoulders as she watched Jacob prepare to head out to the fields.

"Jacob," Poppy called out softly, reluctant to break the stillness of dawn.

He turned, and for a moment, something flickered across his face, and Poppy's heart clenched with a mix of hope and trepidation. He approached her, his boots scuffing the wooden floorboards, and stopped just a breath away.

"Be safe," she murmured.

"Always am," he replied, the hint of a smile ghosting his lips as he leaned down. His kiss was brief, a fleeting press of warmth that filled her with hope. Then he straightened up, the mask of the stoic farmer slipping back into place.

"See you at supper," he said, turning away, the finality in his tone wrapping around Poppy like a shroud.

She watched him walk away, the door closing behind him with a soft click that resounded through the space. Poppy stood motionless, her hand lifting to touch her lips, the ghost of his kiss lingering like a promise—or perhaps a goodbye.

DAYS PASSED, EACH ONE bleeding into the next. The initial spark that had ignited within Poppy's chest began to dim, suffocated by the return of silence and distance. She tried to hold onto the thoughts of their renewed connection, but with no signs it would continue, it dimmed to a distant memory.

Jacob's presence returned to the way it had been before she left, always there and yet unreachable. His conversations were curt, his smiles rare and fleeting. At night, he lay beside her, his breaths steady and even while hers caught in her throat, feeling choked with unshed tears. She would lie awake, listening to the howl of a distant coyote, the rustling of leaves in the wind—and wonder where the man she had married had gone. The vibrant laughter and shared dreams had been replaced by silence.

In her moments of solitude, Poppy gazed out at the sprawling expanse of their homestead. It was a harsh reminder of the reality they faced.

As she stood alone, her hands resting atop the swell of her belly, Poppy realized that survival was a fight to keep the embers of love alive amidst the ashes of grief and responsibility. Whatever it took, she would find a way to get back what they'd lost.

The door creaked behind her as she turned and stepped back into the dimness of the cabin. Poppy was not about to give in to despair. She'd be damned if she let that fire die out without a fight.

Her gaze landed on the small bookshelf that housed the few treasures she had brought from her old life—a well-worn Bible from Sarah, a collection of Shakespearean plays, and a few beloved novels. Literature—the solace of her solitude.

"Words," she whispered to herself, a notion taking root. "Words have power."

The following day, after Jacob left for the fields, Poppy sat at the table, ink and paper before her. With a resolute breath, she began to pen a letter, her handwriting looping gracefully across the page. She wrote of memories, of moments they had shared in laughter and tender whispers. She spoke of her dreams for their child, the future they might build together if only they could bridge the chasm that had opened up between them.

When the letter was done, she folded it carefully and left it atop his pillow. Each day, a new letter waited for him.

Evenings came, and with them, Jacob's return. His dark eyes would flicker with a fleeting spark of curiosity as he found her missives, though he said nothing. But Poppy noticed the subtle shifts—a longer linger in his gaze, a softening around the edges of his stoic demeanor.

She felt it during their silent suppers. And so, she persisted, weaving her love and resolve into every sentence, every plea penned by candlelight.

She invited him to join her on walks, their boots crunching through the new fallen snow.

"Look, Jacob," she'd say softly, her hand resting on his arm as she gestured toward the horizon. "There's so much we haven't seen yet."

And sometimes, just sometimes, she caught the flicker of something in his eyes, a glimmer of the man who had once looked at her as though she were the most wondrous discovery.

Slowly, Poppy chipped away at the walls Jacob had built around himself. She had no illusions—it would take time, effort, perhaps even heartache. But she would slowly rekindle what they had lost.

Chapter Six

Poppy, with her fiery mane of hair secured under a practical bonnet, approached the barn where Jacob was already at work.

"Morning, Jacob," she greeted, tugging her shawl closer around her shoulders against the nip of dawn.

"Poppy," he acknowledged without looking up, his dark hair falling into his eyes as he continued to shovel hay into the stalls.

"Let me help you with that," she offered, rolling up the sleeves of her dress.

Jacob paused, leaning on his pitchfork, watching her with an unreadable expression. "You don't have to do this," he said.

"I know," Poppy replied, her movements deliberate as she picked up a spare pitchfork. "But I want to."

Poppy stole glances at Jacob, noting the set of his jaw, the occasional furrow of his brow when his thoughts turned inward.

"Must've been hard..." Poppy said, breaking the quiet as they moved to the next stall. "Leaving everything behind after the war, starting over."

Jacob's movements slowed, his shoulders tensing beneath the fabric of his worn shirt. "It was necessary," he said after a moment, his voice hushed as if the words were reluctant travelers from his lips.

"Is that why you chose dairy farming?" she asked gently.

A small sigh escaped him, mingling with the earthy scent of the barn. "Wanted something...peaceful," he admitted, his pitchfork piercing the hay with less force than before. "Something that reminded me less of cannons and more of life."

Poppy nodded. She watched as he allowed himself a brief respite, leaning against the wooden wall of the stall, his gaze distant.

"Life has a way of pushing us forward, even when we're not ready to move," she observed softly.

He met her eyes then, and for a fleeting second, she saw the veil lift, revealing a glimpse of the vulnerability he so carefully guarded. "Sometimes, I wish it didn't," Jacob confessed.

Poppy reached out tentatively, her hand brushing against his arm in a gesture of solidarity. "We can't change what's behind us, Jacob. But maybe we can find something worth moving toward."

Jacob's eyes held hers. And in that shared glance, there was an unspoken understanding. His past was filled with hurt, but together they'd try to make their future better.

Later, Poppy and Jacob stood side by side, washing the milk pails at the well. The rhythmic swish of water sloshing against metal was the only sound between them, aside from the occasional snort of a cow from the barn.

"Did you always know you'd become a soldier?" Poppy asked. Her fingers were pruned from the water, but she kept scrubbing, her movements deliberate and mindful.

Jacob paused, his hands stilling over the pail. "My brother and I...we had just lost our parents to a fire. Soldiers were needed and we were both still young enough to think the world of a soldier would be so much better than working in one of the factories."

Poppy saw the subtle tightness in his jaw. She sensed the memories crowding behind his dark eyes. "Your brother," she pressed gently, "you were close?"

"Close as two brothers can be," he replied. He picked up a cloth and resumed wiping the inside of the pail with more vigor than necessary. "I was born fifteen minutes before he was, and I felt like it was my job to take care of him as the older brother. We enlisted together. Promised to watch each other's backs."

"And then...?" Her question hung in the air, tentative yet filled with an earnest desire to understand.

He hesitated, the cloth pausing mid-wipe. "Then Shiloh happened." His voice trembled slightly. "It was chaos—smoke, screams, mud was stained red. We got separated in a charge." Jacob swallowed hard, the muscle in his throat working. "I found him afterward. It was too late." He could still see the accusing look in his brother's eyes as he was dying.

A profound sadness washed over Poppy, seeing the grief that clung to him. She stopped her work, her pail forgotten, and reached out to place a hand over his. "Jacob, I'm so sorry."

For a moment, Jacob looked down at her hand covering his, and something unspoken passed through his expression. "I should have been there," he said, the weight of guilt heavy in his tone. "Should've died instead of him. It feels like him dying allowed me to live."

"Survivor's guilt," Poppy said softly, her heart aching for the man beside her. "But your life—it has a purpose, Jacob. Your brother wouldn't want to see you this lost over his death."

Jacob set the pail down, turning to face her fully, a haunted look in his eyes. "Sometimes it feels like I should have crawled into the coffin beside him. I can't explain what it's like to have an identical twin—someone who is very much a part of you. I feel like I lost half of who I am when he died."

The confession struck Poppy deeply, and she knew this was the source of the walls he had built around himself. Understanding blossomed within her, not just of his pain, but of the immense strength it took to carry such a burden every day.

"Your brother's memory lives on in you, Jacob. I hope you can find peace in knowing you're living for the both of you," she said.

POPPY TRAILED HER FINGERS along the worn wooden fence that enclosed the dairy cows. She stepped closer to Jacob, who was preoccupied with a stubborn calf that refused to nurse, so he was having to bottle-feed it.

"Jacob," she began hesitantly. "I've been thinking about what you shared...and I want you to know you're not alone in carrying burdens."

He paused, the calf momentarily forgotten, his dark eyes flicking toward her. The muscles in his jaw tightened, suggesting he was bracing for words he wasn't sure he wanted to hear.

"During our time on the trail," Poppy continued, "I lost my ma to fever. I was just a girl. My pa...he was never the same. It was like watching him fade away, day by day." Her gaze dropped, focusing on her hands that fidgeted with the hem of her apron. "Sometimes it feels like I failed them both—like I'm still failing. I think Pa was kept alive for as long as he was by the sheer force of Sarah's will. When he died...I think we all wanted to die with him."

The confession hung in the air, heavy and raw. For a moment, Jacob's features softened, and it seemed as if he might reach out. But instead, he turned back to the calf.

"Loss is a part of life, Poppy," Jacob said, his voice terse as he forced the rubber nipple into the calf's mouth. "We all have our crosses to bear."

"Of course," she replied. "But don't you see? Sharing them—it can make the burden lighter."

He shook his head, a bitter chuckle escaping his lips. "Or it can double the weight. Some things are better left buried."

"Even if it means burying a part of yourself?" Poppy pressed. She couldn't accept that as her answer. She needed him to understand she wanted to share his burdens.

"Especially then."

Poppy recoiled slightly, feeling the sting of rejection. She had hoped for a connection, but he was resistant.

"Jacob," she tried again, her words faltering as frustration creased her brow. "I just—"

"Poppy," he interrupted, setting the now-empty bottle aside and facing her. His eyes held a storm within their depths. "I appreciate what you're trying to do, but this isn't a burden I can share with you."

"But you can talk to me about what's happened, and I can understand you better. I know I always feel better when I've shared a problem with someone," she suggested, reaching out a hand, but he moved away from her.

"Poppy..." Jacob's voice trailed off, the struggle evident in his furrowed brow. "Please, just leave it be."

She withdrew her hand, folding her arms across her chest in an unconscious defense. The air grew thick with unspoken words.

"All right, Jacob," Poppy conceded softly, turning away to hide the glimmer of tears that threatened to spill over. "I'll leave it be."

"SARAH," POPPY'S VOICE was barely a whisper, but it carried the weight of her troubled thoughts.

Sarah looked up, her keen eyes quick to notice the shadow that had settled over her sister. "What is it, Poppy?" she asked, setting her sewing aside. Sarah always gave Poppy and her troubles her full attention, which made Poppy feel important. It was something that had helped her through the sadness after the death of their parents.

"It's Jacob," Poppy began. "I fear I've reached the end of what I can do. He's built walls so high around him. I don't know what to do anymore."

"Jacob has been through unimaginable pain," Sarah reminded her gently. "The loss of his brother, the war...those are not easy things to bear, let alone share."

"I know, I do," Poppy said, sinking into a chair opposite Sarah. "But how do I reach him? How do I show him he's not alone, that the burden he carries doesn't have to be his alone to bear?"

Sarah considered her sister, her gaze softening. "Love is a powerful thing, Poppy," she murmured. "But sometimes, love means giving someone the space to heal on their own terms. Just be there for him."

"Do you think he'll ever be happy?" Poppy's hands twisted in her lap. "Or am I just fooling myself, believing that I could be the one to help him find peace?"

"Only Jacob can answer that," Sarah said. "And perhaps, in trying to help him, you'll grow closer. But you may end up pushing him away."

Poppy's eyes filled with unshed tears as the truth of Sarah's words sank in.

THE MORNING SUN HAD scarcely crested the horizon when Poppy found Jacob in the barn. His back was to her, muscles tense as he wrestled with the stubborn lid of a milk churn.

"Jacob?"

He didn't turn, but his shoulders tightened at her approach. "Poppy, what are you doing here so early?"

"Couldn't sleep," she admitted. She drew a steadying breath, the scent of fresh milk and earth grounding her resolve. "Actually, I came to talk."

"Talk?" He turned. The wariness in his stance told Poppy this conversation would not be easy.

"About us," she said, her pulse quickening as she closed the distance between them, mindful of the cows that observed them with mild interest. "I feel like there's a chasm between us, Jacob. One I don't know how to cross."

"Poppy..." His voice was a low rumble of warning.

"Please, hear me out." She pleaded, her hands instinctively reaching for him before she caught herself and let them fall. "I care for you. But sometimes I fear that no matter what I do, it'll never be enough. That your heart... is somewhere I can't reach."

Jacob's jaw clenched, and he turned away, busying himself with the task at hand. "I'm not sure what you want from me. I've got nothing left to give, Poppy. The war...It took everything."

"Everything except your life, Jacob. You're still here, and I believe there's a reason for that." Poppy's voice trembled.

"Is this what you want?!" Jacob exploded suddenly. "To dig up past horrors I've spent years trying to bury?"

"Isn't it exhausting?" She matched his intensity, her own frustrations bubbling to the surface. "Carrying all that pain alone? I just want to help you carry it, Jacob. To share the weight."

"Share the weight?" His laugh was hollow, bitter. "You think love is some kind of magic cure? It's not that simple!"

"Then teach me, Jacob!" Poppy's eyes blazed with the same fiery defiance that mirrored her hair. "Show me how to be there for you, because right now, I feel like I'm grasping at shadows in the dark."

"Maybe that's all we are," he snapped, the words slicing through the tension-charged air. "Shadows of who we once were. You can't save me, Poppy. And I won't drag you into my darkness."

"Then what are we doing?" Her voice cracked, and she wrapped her arms around herself. "What am I to you?"

Jacob's face contorted, and for a moment, she thought he might reach out to her. But then he turned his back once more, leaving her standing alone.

"Surviving," he said simply, the word hanging heavy between them, a finality that echoed in the empty spaces of the barn.

Poppy bit back the sob that threatened to escape, retreating with quiet dignity. As she left the barn, the rift between them felt wider than ever. But within her, a small flame of hope flickered.

POPPY APPROACHED THE fence where Jacob stood alone. His posture was rigid.

"Jacob," she said softly.

He didn't turn to look at her, but his body tensed. The air between them was thick with unspoken words and stifled emotions.

"Where do we go from here?" Poppy asked.

Jacob's hands clenched around the wooden fence, knuckles bleached white. "I don't know, Poppy," he admitted. "I wish I did."

With a sigh that seemed drawn from the very depths of his soul, Jacob turned to face her. In the dimming light, his dark eyes were wells of sorrow.

"Every time I close my eyes, I see it all again...the battlefields, the smoke, the blood." His voice broke. "And Luke... my brother. He was there one moment, alive, and then—"

Poppy watched as Jacob's facade crumbled, the stoic soldier giving way to the grieving twin.

"He should've been the one to live, not me," Jacob confessed. "It was supposed to be me. I was the reckless one, always taking chances. But it was Lucas who was shot. And now, every breath I take feels like I'm stealing it from him."

The weight of his admission hung heavy in the air. Jacob looked lost, a man out of step with time, haunted by a ghost only he could see.

"Is that why you keep everyone at arm's length? Because you think you don't deserve happiness after what happened?" Poppy's voice was gentle, probing the wounds that time had failed to heal.

"Maybe," he said with a shrug. "Or maybe I'm just trying to protect them from the darkness that seems to follow me, even here."

She took a step closer. "We all have shadows, Jacob," she said quietly. "But we also have light. And sometimes, we need someone else to help us find it again."

His eyes met hers, and for a brief moment, the barriers he had erected seemed to waver. "Help me, Poppy," Jacob whispered. "I don't want to be lost anymore."

Poppy took another step toward Jacob and wrapped her arms around him, feeling him stiffen against her. Slowly, though, he relaxed into her embrace, accepting the comfort she was offering.

"Jacob," she said softly, the warmth in her touch bridging the distance between them. Her eyes locked onto his. "You carried this burden alone for so long, but you don't have to anymore. I'm here."

"Every time I close my eyes," Jacob said, "I see him... My brother, falling again and again. And I..." He paused, gathering the shards of his soul scattered by the recollection. "I wonder why it wasn't me."

"Because you're meant to be here, Jacob," Poppy insisted. "Your life—it has purpose."

"Does it?" He searched her face. "Going west was always Lucas's dream. We were supposed to do it together after the war. Of course, he didn't last until after the war."

"I understand." She spoke with assurance. "The past may shape us, but it doesn't define us. We can forge new paths, together."

A heavy sigh escaped him. In the coolness of the impending night, their breaths mingled.

"Poppy," he breathed out her name like a prayer. "I never thought I'd find someone who could understand...someone who could look beyond the scars."

"Scars are just maps of our trials," she whispered back,. "They lead us to places where we can heal, with the help of others."

Their gazes remained locked. "Stay with me tonight," Jacob murmured.

"Always," Poppy replied.

She prayed that his admission that he needed her would lead to the changes necessary for their marriage to continue.

Chapter Seven

Poppy moved through the cabin with a quiet grace, her flaming red hair reflecting the warmth of the hearth. Jacob sat at the rough-hewn table, his dark eyes distant, as he carved away at a piece of wood.

"Would you like some coffee, Jacob?" Poppy asked, her voice gentle. She poured the rich, dark brew into a mug and set it down beside him, her fingers brushing his in a silent offering of love.

Jacob glanced up at her and managed a grateful nod. "Thank you, Poppy," he said. He wrapped his hands around the mug, feeling the heat seep into his skin, and watched as Poppy sat down across from him, socks on the table for her to darn.

"Lucas used to say..." Jacob started, "that coffee was the only reason to get up in the morning." His mouth twitched, a small smile on his face. "He always did appreciate the simple things."

Poppy leaned in, resting her elbow on the table, her face open and attentive. She knew how precious these stories were—tiny windows into the soul of the man she loved. "Tell me more about him," she encouraged, her heart aching for both the man before her and the brother lost.

Jacob's gaze drifted past her. "Lucas was fearless," he said softly. "During the war, he led charges that no one else would. But Lucas believed in our cause enough to risk everything."

Poppy listened, each word etching itself onto her heart. She reached out, her hand finding Jacob's where it rested on the table. She squeezed gently.

"Sometimes I think I can still hear his laugh over the sound of the cattle," Jacob continued. "It's a funny thing...how the mind plays tricks on you."

"Perhaps it's not a trick," Poppy said softly. "Maybe it's a comfort, a reminder that those we love are never truly gone from us."

"Thank you, Poppy," Jacob whispered, the weight of his gratitude palpable. "For listening...for being here."

"Always, Jacob," Poppy replied, her voice steady and sure. "I'm always here."

POPPY EASED THE DOOR shut behind her, the latch clicking with a finality that marked the boundary between Jacob's vulnerability and her solitude. She leaned back against the door for a moment, closing her eyes to gather the tendrils of memory that wove through the quiet room. The stories Jacob had shared about Lucas—a laugh like rolling thunder across the prairie, the way he could charm a smile from even the sternest of faces—flickered in her mind's eye.

She pulled out a sheet of paper and carried it to the table, the quill trembling slightly in her fingers. She knew the importance of capturing the essence of Jacob's words. Each anecdote, each heartfelt remembrance was meticulously transcribed, the ink flowing onto the page.

"Lucas would've loved this place" had been one thing he'd said, whispered as they watched the sun retreat behind the mountains. Poppy had nodded, imagining Lucasbeside them, his spirit as much a part of the land as the soil beneath their feet.

"His strength was unyielding," she wrote now.

"Mrs. Alexander?" The voice, warm and maternal came from the doorway. Mrs. Mitchell stood on the threshold.

"Come in, Mrs. Mitchell," Poppy called, setting aside her writing and rising to greet her visitor.

Mrs. Mitchell entered, her gaze flitting over Poppy's swollen belly before coming to rest on her face. "How are you faring, dear? You're nearly there, aren't you?"

"Eight and a half months," Poppy replied, smoothing her apron over her abdomen. The baby shifted within her, an affirmation of life that both thrilled and terrified her.

"Mercy, but you're as big as the barn," Mrs. Mitchell observed, her tone bordering on admiration and worry. "I hope you're not carrying too much of a burden." Her practiced hands, which had ushered countless new lives into the world, pressed gently against Poppy's middle.

The thawing snow outside had mostly disappeared. Calves stumbled alongside their mothers in the nearby pastures. Poppy felt a kinship with them, bound by the cycle of creation that spared no woman or cow.

"Dr. Bentley says all is well," Poppy assured her. In truth, the weight did seem more than she could bear at times, a heaviness that went beyond the physical.

"Take care, my girl," Mrs. Mitchell said, patting her hand. "I'd like you to go see Dr. Bentley. You're too small to birth a baby of the size you're carrying. We need to make sure you can deliver without his help."

Poppy nodded, feeling the echo of Jacob's fears mingling with her own anticipation. "I'll go see him today."

"I think that's the smartest thing you could do."

Poppy's heart raced with a mix of trepidation and resolve as she made her way to Dr. Bentley's modest clinic on the edge of town.

The door creaked open, and Dr. Bentley welcomed her with a nod. His office was sparse but clean, the smell of antiseptic mingling with the natural scent of pine from the walls. When he spotted her, he called for his wife Betty, who had become his nurse.

"Mrs. Mitchell thinks it might be too big for me to deliver without your assistance," Poppy said as she settled onto the examination table, its leather worn smooth by the anxieties and joys of countless patients before her.

Dr. Bentley offered a kind, if somewhat weary, smile as he retrieved his stethoscope. "Possibly, or it could be twins. Let's have a listen," he said.

Poppy lay back, her hands resting protectively over her swollen belly, her thoughts drifting to Jacob. She imagined him out in the fields and wished he could share in this moment.

The cold metal of the stethoscope pressed against her skin, and she flinched slightly, a small gasp escaping her lips. Dr. Bentley's practiced hands moved deftly, seeking the rhythmic drumming that would confirm or dispel his suspicions.

"Ah," he murmured after a moment. "Two distinct heartbeats. Strong and steady."

Her breath caught in her chest, a swell of emotions flooding her. Twins. The word echoed in her mind, a chorus of joy and fear, a double blessing that brought with it the reminder of Jacob's loss—his twin, Lucas, forever a presence in their lives.

"Thank you, Dr. Bentley," Poppy managed to say, the words thick with unshed tears. She rose from the table, steadied by a newfound sense of purpose.

"Take care now," Dr. Bentley called after her as she stepped outside.

Betty waved to her, having not said a single word during her visit, but Betty had always been more interested in books than people.

As she walked home, she thought of the work that would accompany twins, but she hoped their birth would somehow help Jacob. Her hand rested unconsciously on her belly, envisioning not one, but two new lives entrusted to her care.

Jacob was repairing a fence when she arrived, his dark hair clinging to his forehead. He straightened up as she approached, wiping sweat from his brow with the back of his hand, his dark eyes finding hers.

"Jacob," she said, the excitement bubbling forth, irrepressible. "Dr. Bentley listened, and he heard two heartbeats. Twins, Jacob. We're going to have twins."

His reaction was a tapestry of emotions—astonishment, joy, and an underlying current of fear that she knew all too well.

Jacob stood motionless for a long moment, the news of twins rooting him to the spot. The fence post he had been mending seemed suddenly inconsequential. He looked out over the land that stretched before them, their own slice of promise in this rugged territory.

"Twins," he finally said. "That's...that's remarkable, Poppy."

The smile on her face was radiant. Jacob saw himself reflected in those eyes—a man both bolstered by love and burdened by memories. He knew all too well the bond between twins.

"Are you all right with this, Jacob?" Poppy asked gently, stepping closer to him.

He nodded, the motion sending a few more droplets of sweat to the ground, merging with the soil. "I am," he affirmed, though his brow creased with the gravity of responsibility. "It's just...a lot to take in."

She reached out, her palm warm against his cheek. "We'll take it one day at a time."

That afternoon, Jacob harnessed the horse to the plow, his hooves churning up mud and melting snow. He would make sure Poppy had land ready when she wanted to plant her kitchen garden.

Jacob maneuvered the plow through the rich, dark soil. He glanced back occasionally at the neat furrows, envisioning the vegetables that would soon sprout there, nurtured by Poppy's tender care.

"Looks good, Jacob," Poppy called from where she sat on the porch, a blanket wrapped around her shoulders. Her hands were as busy as ever as she sewed a little gown for one of the babies.

"Good enough for your tomatoes and cucumbers?" he called back.

"Perfect," she replied.

Jacob finished the last row and wiped his brow. The plow rested now at the edge of the freshly turned ground. Jacob leaned against the wooden handle, allowing himself a moment of pride mingled with a prayer for the strength to meet the challenges ahead.

"Come inside," Poppy urged softly. "You've done more than enough for today."

In the quiet that followed, Jacob felt a whisper of peace settle around him. With each step, the fears that clung like burs to his heart loosened ever so slightly. He knew the journey ahead was uncertain, but Jacob also knew one thing for certain—he wouldn't have to walk it alone.

POPPY KNELT IN THE freshly plowed plot, her hands cradling the tender beginnings of what would soon be a vibrant kitchen garden. Each seed she nestled into the soil was a promise for the future. Planting was her favorite part of gardening because it was a new growth and a new beginning.

"Looks like you've got enough green beans there to feed the whole town," Sarah observed with a chuckle, joining her sister amidst the neat rows of planting mounds.

"Jacob did a fine job," Poppy said, brushing a loose strand of red hair from her face. Her fingers felt the earth, cool and yielding, a stark contrast to the swollen tightness of her belly. "He's been... different lately. It's like he's finally finding his way back to himself."

Sarah squatted beside her, her hands mirroring Poppy's motions as they worked side by side, planting seeds that held hope for the coming months. "And how are you feeling about that?"

"Hopeful," Poppy replied, her voice ripe with sincerity. "I see the change in him. It's subtle, but it's there. When he speaks of Lucas now, it's with a kind of peace. It's as if sharing his memories is helping him."

"That's good, Poppy. Real good," Sarah said, her words trailing off as she focused on pressing a kernel of corn into the ground.

The two women continued their quiet labor throughout the day, each lost in thoughts of the past and dreams of what was yet to come.

With dusk came a weariness that settled deep in Poppy's bones. She leaned back against the porch's wooden railing, her hands resting on the swell of her belly. Jacob had come out to join her, watching the horizon swallow the sun with a reverence reserved for the end of hard-won days.

"I feel like the last two months have brought us closer," Poppy said, offering Jacob a smile that spoke of pride and love intertwined.

"Do you now?" Jacob replied, his dark eyes reflecting the twilight. "Well, I'm trying, for you and for them." His gaze dropped to her abdomen, where their future lay hidden beneath layers of fabric and flesh.

As night took hold, Jacob helped Poppy to bed. But sleep proved elusive for Poppy. A pressure building within her, rhythmic and undeniable, whispered of imminent arrival. With each passing moment, the whispers grew into declarations—she was going into labor.

"Jacob," she called. "It's time."

In an instant, the calm of the evening shattered, replaced by the sharp focus of necessity. Jacob sprang into action, his earlier fears subdued by the urgency of the moment.

Jacob's hands shook as he latched the door behind him and plunged into the darkened world beyond their modest homestead.

"Sarah!" he called out as he reached the neighboring cabin, his voice carrying an edge of desperation.

The door swung open, and Sarah stood there, her eyes widening with immediate understanding. She had raised Poppy from a girl; she knew what the late-hour visit signified.

"Poppy?" she asked.

"Going into labor," Jacob managed to say.

"Elmer!" Sarah didn't waste a moment, turning to shout over her shoulder, summoning her husband. Her older children could stay with the younger ones, but she needed to be with her sister.

Elmer King emerged, rubbing sleep from his eyes but snapping to attention at the sight of Jacob's expression.

"Go for Dr. Bentley and Mrs. Mitchell. Now, Elmer!" Sarah's directions were swift, her tone leaving no room for question.

Without a word, Elmer grabbed his coat and hat, the weariness gone from his face. He vanished into the night, the crunch of his boots fading as he set out on his errand.

"Come," Sarah said softly. "You're no use to Poppy fretting outside. Let's get you back to her."

Together, they retraced Jacob's frantic steps beneath a sky sprinkled with uncaring stars. Sarah's presence was both a comfort and a reminder of the weight of responsibility resting on Jacob's shoulders. Inside, Poppy was fighting her own battle.

As they entered the warm glow of the cabin, Jacob's gaze landed once again on his wife, her face etched with both pain and determination. He took his place beside her, his hand finding hers, their fingers intertwining.

Chapter Eight

Jacob stood in the cramped confines of the log cabin, his dark eyes fixed on the curtained-off corner where his wife labored. His hands, rough and calloused from years of farming, clenched and unclenched at his sides. The air was thick with anticipation and the musky scent of wood smoke. He could hear Poppy's muffled cries, and he cringed each time.

The door swung open with a creak that seemed to echo through the silence, and Mrs. Mitchell bustled in, her no-nonsense demeanor slicing through the tension. "Out you go, Jacob," she commanded, swooping into the room with the confidence of a woman who had ushered countless new lives into the world. "Childbirth is no place for a man, especially not a fretting father-to-be."

Jacob's jaw tightened. "Mrs. Mitchell, I want to be here for Poppy," he said, his voice a low rumble of protest. It was his responsibility, his duty, to stand by his wife's side, just as he had stood by his brother's until the very end.

"Jacob," Mrs. Mitchell said, placing her hands firmly on her ample hips, "you'll do your wife more good by giving her space to bring those babes into the world. Now off with you to the barn. There's work to be done, isn't there?"

There was indeed. The second cradle awaited him—a symbol of survival and the future. With one last look toward the curtain, Jacob nodded.

He trudged out of the cabin and toward the barn.

Inside, the scent of fresh-cut hay mingled with the earthy aroma of sawdust. Jacob approached the half-finished cradle, running his fingers over the smooth curves of the wood.

He picked up the sandpaper, the grit biting into his skin as he began to work with rhythmic strokes. The motion was methodical allowing his mind to drift to what lay ahead. The sound of sanding filled the barn, punctuated by the occasional distant cry from the cabin.

As the wood beneath his hands grew sleeker and the unfinished cradle took shape, Jacob imagined the tiny forms that would soon rest within its embrace. He envisioned nights spent rocking his children to sleep, days watching them grow strong under the vast expanse of sky. In the smoothing of the wood, he sought to carve out a semblance of control.

Sarah moved with quiet haste around the modest cabin, her hands shaking slightly as she stoked the fire and set a pot of water to boil. She knew from her own experience with childbirth that boiling water before they used it would keep the mother and infants from getting infections.

Her sister, Poppy, lay upon the bed, a quilt hand-stitched by their late mother bunched beneath her. Poppy's breaths were shallow, her freckled face glistening with sweat, strands of fiery red hair clinging to her forehead. Sarah wiped Poppy's brow with a damp cloth, offering a silent prayer to the sturdy fabric that had mopped up tears, blood, and the sweat of fevered brows through so many seasons.

"Keep her calm," Mrs. Mitchell instructed. "And keep that water coming."

The door shuddered open, and Dr. Bentley stepped inside, his presence immediately filling the room with a different kind of weight. His eyes, dark and steady, swept over the scene before him, taking in every detail—the pallor of Poppy's skin, the determined set of Mrs. Mitchell's shoulders, the simmering pot of water. He carried with him a satchel of instruments and an air of readiness.

"Let's hope I'm only here for reassurance," he said, his voice low and even as he set down his bag and rolled up his sleeves. "But we'll be ready for whatever comes."

"Thank you, Doctor," Sarah murmured, turning back to tend to the kettle as another contraction seized Poppy, drawing a sharp cry from her lips.

JACOB'S HANDS WERE coarse with wood shavings, the rhythmic scrape of the sandpaper against the oak cradle a meditative mantra that kept his rising panic at bay. Each stroke was a silent prayer for Poppy and the life she was bringing into the world. The barn had become his sanctuary, a place to channel his helplessness into labor.

As he smoothed down an edge, the barn door creaked open, admitting both a gust of the evening chill and Elmer King's sturdy frame. Without a word, Elmer took up position on the other side of the cradle, picking up a piece of sandpaper and joining Jacob in his work.

"You don't have to stay, Elmer," Jacob said after a time, his voice barely above the whisper of sandpaper on wood. "The night is growing cold. Your family will worry."

Elmer paused, looking up from the curved rail he was smoothing. "I've got a stake in waiting, same as you," he replied, his voice carrying the weight of unspoken history. "Poppy's like my own kin. I helped raise her after all. And that child—," he corrected himself gently, "it'll be my blood too, in a way."

Jacob nodded, acknowledging the bond that tied them together.

"Thank you," was all Jacob could say, the gratitude profound but the ability to express it difficult through the tightness in his throat.

"Nothing to thank me for," Elmer responded, returning to his task as if the rhythm of their work could somehow make the labor easier for Poppy.

And so, in silence punctuated only by the occasional groan of settling wood and the distant echo of a coyote's howl, two men sanded a cradle for a new life.

Jacob worked with an intensity that mirrored the resolve he'd carried since the war. Elmer stood across from him, his hands moving in tandem with Jacob's, both focused on the task at hand, shaping the cradle that would hold not one future, but two.

"Elmer," Jacob finally broke the silence, pausing to inspect a particularly stubborn knot in the pine. "It's children not child. Poppy's having twins."

Elmer's sanding slowed, then stopped. He looked up, his eyes reflecting the flickering lantern light, a trace of surprise registering before settling back into the worn lines of his face. "Twins, huh?" he said, the corners of his mouth lifting just slightly. "Well, that's double the blessing—and double the trouble."

A faint smile tugged at Jacob's lips, acknowledging the truth in Elmer's words. He and his brother had once embodied the idea of twins being double trouble.

"Double the worry right now," Jacob admitted, turning back to the cradle.

They returned to their work, the silence settling over them once more.

Hours passed, though they seemed like weeks, and then the door swung open, casting Sarah's slender silhouette against the night sky.

"Jacob, Elmer," she called softly, her voice threading through the stillness. "You best come now."

Both men straightened, the urgency in Sarah's tone snapping them out of their concentrated labor. They exchanged a glance, tools abandoned as they brushed sawdust from their clothes and made their way toward the house, hearts heavy with anticipation for the news that awaited them.

Jacob's boots thudded softly against the dirt as he approached the cabin, each step heavy with trepidation. The door creaked open, and he paused.

Inside, the air was thick with the scent of sweat and wood smoke. A low-burning flame in the hearth cast flickering shadows across the room, revealing Poppy propped up against a stack of pillows. Her flaming red hair lay damp against her flushed cheeks. She looked exhausted, but he could see the happiness in her eyes.

Jacob's breath caught in his throat as he took in the tableau before him—Poppy cradling not one, but two small bundles at her breast. Each child, a mirror image of peace, their tiny heads crowned with tufts of dark hair that hinted at their father's lineage.

"Jacob..." Poppy's voice was a whisper, yet it cut through the silence like the call of a meadowlark. "Meet your sons."

He edged closer, the floorboards groaning beneath his weight as if sharing the burden of his sudden rush of emotions. His gaze shifted between the infants, taking in every detail—the curve of their rosebud lips, the gentle rise and fall of their chests.

"Two boys," she continued, her words laced with a hint of laughter and wonder. "I think... I think we should call them Luke and Jake."

The names echoed in Jacob's mind, each syllable a promise, an anchor to the future they would build together in this untamed land.

"Luke and Jake," Jacob repeated softly, the sound of their names settling around him like a benediction. "We were Lucas and Jacob." He reached out, his fingers trembling as they brushed against the downy softness of his children's heads. At that moment, the weight of his past sorrows seemed to lift ever so slightly, making room for a hope that surged within him.

Jacob's knees nearly buckled with the force of his emotions as he pulled a wooden chair closer to the bed, its legs scraping against the plank floor. He sank down, his gaze never leaving the tiny faces nestled against Poppy's chest. "Luke...Jake," he murmured, feeling that it was right. He nodded, once, decisively. "Yes, Luke and Jake."

"Look at them, Jacob," Poppy whispered. "They have your dark hair, your strength even now."

He could only nod again, his throat tight with unshed tears. The lives they had brought forth were a balm to the scars left by war and loss. These boys, his sons, were the future.

"We'll teach them to ride and to read the land," Jacob said, his voice rough with emotion. "They'll grow up strong and free here, without the shadow of war looming over them."

"And kind," Poppy added, her eyes shining with hope.

"Kind," he echoed, picturing two young boys learning the ways of the trail, their laughter ringing out as they discovered the world around them. A world he would shape into a sanctuary for them, a place where the ghosts of his past could not reach.

"Promise me, Jacob," Poppy said, her hand reaching out to clasp his, "that whatever comes, we'll handle it together."

"Nothing could pull me away from you or our sons," he vowed. "We're bound by our sons."

Jacob reached out a trembling hand, his fingertips brushing against the downy softness of a small head. The infant's skin was warm, pulsing with new life under his touch. He hadn't realized how much room there was in his heart until this moment—until these tiny beings had filled it to brimming.

"Hey there," he whispered.

The baby turned slightly at the sound, nuzzling instinctively in the crook of his arm. Jacob felt a surge of protectiveness that was even stronger than the loyalty he had known for his brother.

In the quiet of the cabin, with dawn's light meandering across the wooden floorboards, the world narrowed to the confines of this room. Here, the weight of the past seemed to lift from Jacob's shoulders as he cradled his son, the future embodied in miniature breaths and the gentle curve of rosebud lips.

He allowed himself to trace the delicate eyebrows of the other boy, a mirror image of the first, sleeping soundly beside his twin. It struck him then, the enormity of it all, the responsibility of shaping these new lives.

"Luke...Jake..." he murmured, testing the names on his tongue, a solemn vow etched into each syllable. "My boys."

Tears gathered at the corners of his eyes, unbidden yet unashamed in their descent. They were tears born not from sorrow, but from an overwhelming sense of love.

"Look at you," Poppy's voice was a soft lullaby, her gaze locked onto their sons with pride and wonder. "Strong already, just like your pa."

"Strong, and so much more." Jacob responded. "I'll teach them to be free, like the river that carves its own path."

"Free," Poppy echoed, a smile touching her lips.

"Free," he affirmed, holding his sons close.

Here, Jacob Alexander, former soldier, and now father, found redemption in the simplest act of love. Just touching them, he was deeply, irrevocably in love with them.

Chapter Nine

Poppy cradled one of the twins in the crook of her arm, the other nestled against her chest. Motherhood was filled with so many emotions: boundless joy and relentless responsibility stretching out before her. The love she felt for these two boys was fierce, a protective surge that both uplifted and exhausted her.

She moved about the wooden cabin, her feet whispering across the rough-hewn floorboards. The fireplace crackled, the only sound other than the soft cooing of the infants. She gathered soiled diapers, a never-ending cycle of wash and wear, and soaked them in a basin of hot water, scrubbing until her knuckles turned red and raw.

With each passing day, she felt a little more overwhelmed. Each diaper wrung out was a reminder of the ceaseless duties that motherhood entailed. Poppy paused, holding a dripping cloth to her chest, and sighed.

"Motherhood is the school of hard knocks, isn't it my darlings?" she whispered to the boys, who simply gazed back with wide, curious eyes. They were her pupils now, her most important and challenging students.

She hung the diapers near the fire, their white forms stark against the dark wood of the cabin walls. As they dried, stiff and clean, Poppy stood by the window, watching the sunrise.

POPPY'S HANDS MOVED methodically, pulling weeds from the garden, her fingers stained with earth. The sun bore down on her back as she worked, the broad brim of her bonnet casting a shadow over the twin basket beside her. Inside, her boys slept soundly, oblivious to the symphony of life buzzing around them. She glanced at them often, their peaceful slumber reassuring her weary heart.

"Rest now, little ones," she murmured as she returned to her task, "for the world will ask much of you."

Each day that passed brought her sister, Sarah, offering help for Poppy with her new sons. With every visit, Sarah brought with her a wellspring of knowledge and comfort, teaching Poppy how to soothe colic and swaddle a restless infant.

"Let them feel the breeze, Poppy. It's good for them, and it'll be good for you too," Sarah had advised, placing the twins gently into a wicker basket one afternoon.

And so, Poppy learned to balance her roles as a mother and a wife, making sure her husband felt loved just as much as her sons did.

"Are they cozy out here?" Jacob would ask each evening as he approached from the fields. His eyes now shone with a tenderness reserved only for his family.

"Cozy as can be," Poppy would reply, looking up from the garden with a soft smile.

"Let me take over here. How are you feeling?" His words were simple, yet they carried the strength of mountains, the compassion of a man who had known loss and now cherished every breath of life before him.

"Overwhelmed," she confessed some days, her flaming red hair clinging to her damp forehead. "But grateful."

"Then let's be overwhelmed together," Jacob would say, kneeling beside her to weed the garden, his hands mirroring her own. And in those moments, the burdens of their world seemed lighter.

As dusk fell upon the homestead, Poppy would watch Jacob with their sons, marveling at the gentle giant he became in their presence.

He cradled their tiny bodies with a careful grace, his rough hands softened by the touch of innocence.

"Anything else I can do?" he'd ask every night without fail, a glass of milk from their cows in hand, offering sustenance for both body and spirit.

"Just keep being you," Poppy would answer. They were partners on this trail of life, navigating its twists and turns.

POPPY SAT IN THE WEATHERED rocking chair her sister had passed down to her, her fingers brushing over the soft, downy heads of her sons as they slept. Her heart was a tapestry of love and worry, each thread meticulously woven with the whisper of their breaths.

Jacob leaned against the doorway, his dark eyes lost in thought. He watched Poppy with an affection that seemed to fill the room, spilling into every corner like the warmth from their stove.

"Lucas and I used to dream about this," he began softly, breaking the silence. "A home...family..." His voice trailed off, but she felt the weight of his unspoken words heavy in the air between them.

"Tell me more," Poppy urged. Every time he talked about Lucas, he seemed to feel a bit better about the past.

He took a seat beside her, the floorboards creaking under his weight, and sighed. "New York was nothing like this." A ghost of a smile played upon his lips as he reminisced. "Lucas and I, we were inseparable. Even folks who knew us well had trouble telling us apart." He chuckled, the sound rich with nostalgia. "We had our ways to make sure we never went hungry. Holding horses' reins for pennies, running errands...We looked out for each other."

Poppy listened intently, each detail painting a picture in her mind of the young boys hustling through the bustling streets of a city so unlike the open skies they lived under now. She imagined Jacob and

Lucas, two halves of a whole, bound by the kind of love she wanted for her own children.

"Promise me," she whispered, her gaze moving to the peaceful expressions of their slumbering boys, "promise me they'll know that same bond."

"I promise," he said, the vow a solemn pledge to the past and future alike.

TIME PASSED, MEASURED not by the ticking of a clock but by the growth of their sons, until the day came when the boys reached their six-week milestone. The land around them bloomed with the promise of spring, yet the shadow of winter's flu still lingered, a stark reminder of the fragility of life on the frontier.

Dressed in their Sunday best, Poppy cradled one son while Jacob carefully wrapped the other in a blanket, both parents wearing expressions of quiet pride. They stepped outside, the fresh air a balm after weeks of seclusion, and made their way to the church.

"Are you ready for this?" Jacob asked, his hand finding hers, their fingers intertwining.

"Ready as I'll ever be," Poppy replied, the flutter in her stomach a mix of nerves and excitement. She'd had no idea she would be nervous taking her babies to church for the first time.

With careful steps, they entered the house of worship, the congregation turning to greet the newest members of their community. Poppy's heart swelled as she saw the mix of smiles and nods directed their way, each a silent prayer of welcome and well-being.

As they settled into a pew, Pastor Scott's voice rose and fell with the cadence of scripture, yet it was the sight of her small family together in God's eye that filled Poppy with a profound sense of peace.

POPPY SAT IN THE CREAKING rocker, the soft suckling sounds of her boys nursing the only noise breaking the silence of the room. Her back ached with the strain of motherhood, and her eyes drooped with the weight of sleepless nights, yet as she gazed upon the tiny faces of her sons, a rush of warmth flooded her weary heart.

Jacob stood in the doorway, watching the scene with a tenderness that softened the hard lines of his face—a face that had seen too much loss and sorrow in recent years. He stepped quietly, mindful not to disturb the sacred ritual before him, and approached with a glass brimming with milk. It was rich and creamy.

"Here," he said gently, offering the glass to Poppy. "They say it's good for you—will help you keep up your strength."

Poppy paused to take the glass, her lips curving into a grateful smile as she sipped the fresh milk. "Thank you, Jacob," she murmured.

His hand lingered on her shoulder in a silent vow of support, his presence a constant like the mountains framing their valley—a reminder of the steadfastness required to survive here. As Poppy resumed feeding the twins, Jacob watched over them, his thoughts wandering to his own twin brother, Lucas, whose memory was a bittersweet ache within his chest.

The creak of the door announced the arrival of Elmer and Sarah. They entered bearing gifts—a pair of small rocking chairs, expertly crafted, and a dresser with enough drawers to hold tiny garments and precious mementos. The furniture was simple, yet each piece was imbued with the love and hope of family.

"Look at these little fellas," Elmer exclaimed, his voice a rumble of joy as he reached out to cradle one of the boys for the first time. His large, calloused hands enveloped the infant with surprising gentleness, and his eyes sparkled with unspoken dreams. "My grandsons," he said, his voice catching with emotion.

Sarah moved beside Poppy, her sisterly bond woven through years of shared trials and triumphs. She smiled down at her sister and the babes with pride, her assistance over the past weeks having been needed more than Poppy had ever imagined.

As the evening light waned, the cabin filled with the quiet chatter of family, the exchange of stories, and the laughter that comes from hearts intertwined by blood and marriage.

Poppy stood, her arms enveloping Sarah in a heartfelt embrace. "I don't know how I would have made it through without you," she murmured, her voice thick with gratitude. A stray wisp of her flaming red hair brushed against Sarah's cheek.

"Ah, don't mention it, sis," Sarah said, her own voice catching as she pulled back just enough to look into Poppy's eyes. "You've done the same for me." Elmer watched them.

Poppy turned toward him, her gaze softened by affection. "And you, Elmer," she began, her hand reaching out to rest on his forearm, "your kindness has been a constant in my life, and I thank you for it." The words were simple, yet they carried the weight of their shared journey, the miles traversed, and the hardships borne together.

Elmer gave a humble nod, his eyes crinkling at the corners. "Family takes care of each other, Poppy. That's what we do."

As the couple departed, Poppy could not help but feel the ties of kinship pulling taut around her heart. She had the best upbringing an orphan could ask for with Sarah and Elmer, and she would always be grateful.

Now alone, Poppy and Jacob sat side by side, the silence between them filled with the soft cooing of their sons. Jacob's dark eyes, always so full of strength and resolve, now held a gentle light as he watched over their sleeping boys. The pensive set of his jaw seemed to melt away as memories stirred within him.

"Poppy," he began, "did I ever tell you about the time Lucas and I would hold horses for folks in the city?" His eyes danced with the flicker of recollection. "We'd offer to watch them while people bustled about their business in the shops. Earned us a few coins, and we were always so proud to give them to our mother."

She leaned closer, smiling. The image of Jacob as a boy, his hands gripping the reins tightly, emerged vividly in her mind's eye.

"From dawn till dusk, after school hours, we'd find whatever work was going," he continued, a smile tugging at the corner of his mouth. "Even as children, we knew the value of hard work."

"Seven years old, you say?" Poppy whispered.

"Seven years old," Jacob confirmed, his gaze shifting from the past to the present—to the two small lives before them that held the promise of tomorrow. "But Lucas and I, we had each other. And I want that for our boys too."

In the stillness of the cabin, with the embers of the day fading outside, Poppy felt the threads of grief and loss entwined with those of love and hope. Here, in this new world they were forging together, survival meant more than merely existing—it meant building a legacy of brotherhood and unity.

Chapter Ten

Poppy spent the day of her wedding anniversary washing diapers and working in the garden. She changed into clean clothes before Jacob was due to come home, but she was certain he'd forgotten, which was all right with her. So much had happened in their year together that it surprised her to realize it truly had only been one year.

Just before Jacob arrived at the end of his workday, Sarah, Elmer, and their children arrived. Poppy was surprised to see the children with them because they hadn't spent much time at her new home. Not that she minded. She'd taught her nephews and nieces in school, and she had a close relationship with each of them.

"What are you doing here?" Poppy asked. "I was just about to put supper on the table."

"We're here to take care of the boys while you and Jacob go to supper at the boarding house. Happy anniversary, little sister." Sarah spread her arms, embracing Poppy. "It's been a tough first year for you, but I have a feeling everything will be better from this moment forward."

"Are you sure Jacob is planning to take me out for supper?" Poppy asked, surprised to hear he'd remembered their anniversary.

Sarah nodded. "We're eating your supper. I brought two loaves of bread and a dessert, so we can stretch whatever you made into a meal for all of us."

Poppy smiled. "I made a beef stew with dumplings. It's Jacob's favorite."

"I'm sure we'll enjoy it then," Elmer said, grinning at her.

"I've never left the babies..." Poppy said. "I nursed them a few minutes ago though."

"They'll be fine until you get home then. If they start crying, we'll send Herman to fetch you." Herman was Sarah and Elmer's oldest son.

"I don't mind, Aunt Poppy!"

Poppy smiled. "I suppose the decision is made then."

Jacob opened the door to the cabin then. "Are you ready?" he asked.

Poppy nodded. Apparently, Jacob had kept a change of clothes in the barn because his clothes weren't covered in sweat and dirt. "I'm ready. I'm not ready to leave my sons, but I'm ready to spend time alone with my husband."

The team was hitched to the buggy, and Jacob helped her inside. "The boys will be fine," Jacob told her. She knew they would, but it was still a little scary to leave them.

"When did you plan all this?" she asked.

"Last week," he said. "When I realized our anniversary was close, I decided that I needed a bit of time with my wife."

He guided the buggy toward town. "I wish I had time to take you for a drive to the lake today, but that'll wait until the weekend. The boys should get to see it too."

She laughed softly. The boys were two months old and didn't particularly care about seeing the lake, but she would be happy to make the drive with him. "That sounds wonderful."

Jacob had been a changed man since the boys were born, and she was thrilled that he was treating her as she'd expected to be treated when they first married. It was strange that he wanted private time with her, even though he'd ignored her for a long time when they were newlyweds.

At the boarding house, Margaret herself brought their meals out to them. She handed Jacob some flowers, and he in turn, presented them to Poppy. "I didn't have time to pick any today, but I asked Margaret to have some ready for you."

Poppy smiled, burying her face in the blooms. "Thank you."

Jacob tilted his head to one side. "Your smile is thanks enough."

She tried a bite of the food Margaret had brought and smiled. "I wish I could cook as well as Margaret."

"Oh, you cook every bit as well as she does." He took a bite of the pot roast in front of them. "I prefer the way you season your roast."

"You've changed," she said softly.

He took a deep breath and looked into her eyes. "Having the twins, and them both being boys named after Lucas and me...I feel like I get to have a second chance to make things right, if that makes any sense at all."

Poppy nodded. "I think it does."

He smiled. "And watching you with the boys, and seeing how you care for them, the same way you care for me...I love you, Poppy. I took way too long to say it, and I feel like I let you down in so many ways. But it's true. And once I love, I never let go." He reached for her hand and drew it to his lips. "Thank you for not giving up on me."

Poppy sniffled, tears falling down her cheeks. "I've waited so long to hear you say that. I love you as well. I am so glad you're the man I'm spending my life with."

"I couldn't be happy without you."

Epilogue

Poppy, her flaming red hair tied back in a practical braid, stepped out onto the porch of the farmhouse she shared with Jacob and their seven children, a steaming cup of coffee cradled between her hands. She inhaled deeply, the crisp air mingling with the earthy scent of the livestock.

Jacob joined her, wrapping an arm around her waist. His touch was a quiet reminder of the bond they shared. He was happy that he'd found a way to keep going in the arms of the woman beside him.

"Morning, darling," he murmured.

"Morning," Poppy replied, leaning into his embrace. "Looks like it's going to be another beautiful day."

They stood together in comfortable silence, watching as the world awakened around them. It was in these moments that they allowed themselves to reflect, not only on the sorrows of their past but also on the profound gratitude they felt for their present. The farm was their sanctuary, a place where they could navigate the ebb and flow of life side by side.

"Shall we start with the southern pasture today?" Poppy asked.

"Sounds good," Jacob agreed, the corners of his eyes crinkling with the affectionate smile he reserved for his wife. "I'll fetch the tools."

With a gentle squeeze of her shoulder, he kissed her temple before stepping off the porch, his movements deliberate and filled with purpose. He had taken to farming with a dedication that spoke of his desire to provide, to nurture the land as much as it nurtured him and his family.

Poppy watched him go, pride swelling in her chest. Maybe the first year of her marriage had been difficult, but now she loved every minute of her daily routine. She worked to find joy in everything around her. It was there in the way Jacob paused to look back at her, his eyes shining with unspoken love, and in the way she lifted her hand to wave, her heart full and content.

IN THE SIMPLE ACTS of living and working their farm, Poppy and Jacob had discovered a romance that made life worth living and made them want to live long lives filled with love.

"Morning, Bessie," Jacob greeted the nearest cow, a gentle giant with soulful brown eyes. She mooed softly in response, familiar with the daily ritual.

Poppy set the pails down and began to prepare Bessie for milking, her hands practiced and efficient. She leaned her head against the cow's warm flank. It was a comforting reminder of their shared existence—of lives intertwined with the land and the animals they cared for.

"Remember how skittish she was when we first got her?" Poppy's voice was soft, almost lost amidst the sounds of the barn.

Jacob chuckled, casting a glance her way. "Like you with your first classroom of students."

"Seems like we've all settled in nicely," she replied, the corners of her mouth lifting slightly.

"We have." Jacob's agreement came with the subtle acknowledgment of the hardships they'd faced. His fingers worked deftly on another cow, squeezing milk into the waiting pail with a rhythmic squirt that harmonized with Poppy's efforts.

Poppy stood, wiping her hands on her apron. "I'll start breakfast."

"Let me finish up here," Jacob said, nodding toward the remaining cows. He watched her depart, never tiring of admiring her.

Inside the farmhouse, the aroma of coffee percolated through the kitchen as Poppy stoked the fire in the stove. She cracked eggs with a precise tap against the rim of the bowl, their golden yolks a vibrant contrast to the whites. She put the bacon in the frying pan, standing over it, ready to turn the pieces.

From the window over the sink, she could see Jacob scattering feed for the chickens, his movements deliberate.

By the time he returned to the house, scrubbing his hands clean at the basin outside, the table was laden with food. Poppy waited, her hands folded in front of her, the lines of her face softening as she watched him cross the threshold. There was no need for words—their life spoke volumes in the quiet moments, in the sharing of burdens, and in the breaking of bread together.

"Looks perfect," Jacob remarked, taking his seat and reaching for her hand. Their fingers entwined naturally, a silent prayer of thanks offered for the day ahead, for the love that sustained them.

The morning meal concluded with the soft clatter of utensils and the scrape of chairs against the worn wooden floor. Seven pairs of young eyes shone with eagerness, reflecting the flame of the hearth and the warmth that filled the farmhouse. Poppy rose from her chair to gather the dishes. But before she could reach for the first plate, Jacob's firm yet gentle hand on her arm halted her.

"Let the moments linger," he said. "There's no rush, Poppy."

She nodded, the corners of her mouth lifting in agreement as she sank back down, allowing herself to be enveloped by the cacophony of their children's laughter and chatter. They were stories in motion, tales spun from the fabric of their everyday lives. Little Elijah, with his father's dark eyes, regaled his siblings with exaggerated tales of his imaginary encounters with wild coyotes, while the twins, Luke and Jake, acted out each scene with dramatic flair.

"Pa! Pa!" the youngest, Benjamin, barely four years old, tugged insistently at Jacob's sleeve, his cherubic face upturned, eyes sparkling with the anticipation of attention. "Me ride horse today?"

Jacob ruffled his son's chestnut curls, a soft smile gracing his lips. "Maybe later, Benji," he promised. The memory of his brother, lost in battle so far from these lush green fields, flickered across his mind. But here, in the presence of his family, the darkness of loss was always pushed back by the light of new life and laughter.

"Come now, children," Poppy chimed in, her teacher's voice a tender melody amidst the din. "We've chores awaiting us, and I'll need all hands on deck."

They scattered, each child heading toward their appointed tasks with a sense of purpose instilled by their parents. Jake and Luke led the way to the chicken coop, their steps synchronized with the unspoken understanding of shared responsibility. They moved with care, collecting eggs with a gentleness, placing each precious orb into wicker baskets lined with straw.

"Like Ma says, treat them as you would a newborn babe," Elizabeth reminded her twin sister, Sarah, her words echoing the lessons imparted by Poppy's steady guidance.

"Got it, Lizzy," Sarah replied.

Poppy watched from the kitchen window, her heart swelling, and not just from the sight of her children embracing their duties. There was Jacob, amongst the cows, guiding little Rebecca's hands as she grasped the teat of Bessie, their most patient milk cow.

"Easy now, Becky," he coaxed, "just like this." His hands moved in tandem with hers.

"Love's work is never done," Poppy mused aloud, though there was no sorrow in her reflection.

POPPY'S SKIRTS SWISHED softly as she padded across the grassy bank, her eyes lingering on the scene unfurling before her. The creek murmured in a gentle serenade, its waters cool and inviting as her children splashed with wild abandon. Jacob stood at the water's edge, his trousers rolled up to his knees, a smile softening the hard lines etched by years of war and work.

"Be mindful of the little ones," Poppy called out, her voice carrying over the bubbling currents. The creek was filled with all the people she loved most in this world, and she couldn't imagine her life any other way.

"Always am, my dear," Jacob replied without looking back, his attention dedicated to the youngest, Benjamin, who clutched a pebble with determination written on his small face.

Under the shade of the ancient oak tree, a red-and-white checkered blanket was spread out, laden with sandwiches, fresh milk, and apple pies—remnants of the morning's labor transformed into a feast. Poppy watched their seven children, their joy untamed as the land surrounding them. She felt Jacob beside her now, his presence a constant comfort.

"Days like these..." Jacob started, his voice trailing off, but Poppy knew the unspoken words. They were days of pure contentment, and they had them as often as life would allow.

Later, the children gathered around Jacob, who had fetched Duchess, their gentlest mare. His hands offered guidance to small fingers gripping reins. He lifted Rebecca onto the horse's back, her tiny frame steadied by his sure touch.

"Keep your back straight, and don't grip too tight," he instructed, his words measured, his own experiences of riding through the chaos of battle transforming into lessons of grace and balance.

ON THE PORCH SWING, Poppy's skirt whispered against the weathered wood as she swayed gently beside Jacob. His dark hair had begun to silver at the temples, and he looked very distinguished.

"Remember the first time we watched a sunset together?" she asked.

Jacob's hand found hers, his fingers intertwining with her own—a touch that spoke volumes of shared hardship and triumph. "How could I forget? The world seemed to stand still, just for us."

The front door creaked open, spilling warm lamplight onto the porch. One by one, their children emerged, their faces sleepy yet content.

"Goodnight, Mama. Goodnight, Papa," they chimed, their voices mingling in the evening air.

Each child approached, offering hugs that clung like burrs and kisses that held the sweetness of molasses. Jacob ruffled hair and wrapped his arms around small shoulders. Poppy kissed foreheads, whispering to each child of their accomplishments of the day.

"Sleep tight, my darlings," Poppy called softly as they scampered back inside, her heart swelling with a love as vast as the frontier they had conquered.

"Look at us, Jacob," Poppy said, her voice barely above a whisper, "Look what we've created together."

"A thriving farm and many children to love with all our hearts."

Rising from the porch swing, Poppy took Jacob's hand, her fingers tracing the calluses. They stepped through the farmhouse door, leaving behind the whispers of night to enter the sanctuary of their shared solitude. The bedroom, with its quilt-covered bed and the flickering flame of a single candle, welcomed them into its warm embrace.

Jacob closed the door with a soft click, his eyes never leaving Poppy's. The world beyond their walls, with its endless responsibilities and memories of loss, seemed to fade in the presence of this intimate space. He brushed a stray lock of hair from her face, tucking it gently behind her ear. In that simple gesture lay the depth of understanding they had cultivated like the crops in their fields—tended with care, weathered by storms, and stronger for it.

"Every day with you is a gift," Jacob murmured. Their bodies knew each other's rhythms, fitting together as seamlessly as the melody of a well-loved song.

Poppy leaned into his chest, her breath syncing with his heartbeat. "And every night," she replied, her hands resting on his broad shoulders, "is a chance to share our love."

They undressed each other, each article of clothing dropped to the wooden floor. Clad only in the vulnerability of their skin, they slid between the cool sheets, seeking the warmth of their entwined bodies.

"Remember when..." Jacob started, his voice trailing off as if hesitant to disturb the sanctity of their reminiscence.

"Every moment," Poppy assured him, squeezing his hand.

9 798224 538508